CAPTAIN NAVARRE

THE SCIENCE OFFICER
VOLUME 12

BLAZE WARD

KNOTTED ROAD PRESS

Captain Navarre
The Science Officer Volume 12
Blaze Ward
Copyright © 2022 Blaze Ward
All rights reserved
Published by Knotted Road Press
www.KnottedRoadPress.com

ISBN: 978-1-64470-279-6

Cover art:
Illustration 52662783 / Alien © Philcold | Dreamstime.com

Cover and interior design copyright © 2022 Knotted Road Press

Reviews
It's true. Reviews help. Even a short one, such as, "Loved it!" So please consider reviewing this book (and all of the ones you've read) on your favorite retailer site.

Never miss a release!
If you'd like to be notified of new releases, sign up for my newsletter.

http://www.blazeward.com/newsletter/

Buy More!
Did you know that you can buy directly from my website?

https://www.blazeward.com/shop/

ALSO BY BLAZE WARD

Start with: Mirrors

Fairchild

Start with: Fairchild

Last Stand

Start with: Lost Dreams

The Lazarus Alliance

Start with: Escape

Shadow of the Dominion

Start with: Longshot Hypothesis

Star Dragon

Start with: Birth of the Star Dragon

Kincaide's War

Start with: The Eden Package

Star Tribes

Start with: Winterstar

ACTION-ADVENTURE

Pacific Force

Start with: Pacific Force

The Red Branch

Start with: Night Strike

Swordmistress Zhen

Start with: Traveler From The West

FANTASTICAL

The Gunderson Case Files, Volume 1

Augustus Derlyth, Occult Detective

Start with: Ill Tidings

CONTENTS

OUTBOUND

SYNTHA

KOVALEV'S PALACE

SURAYYA

CAPTAIN NAVARRE

NINOVSKAYA

PART 1

Zakhar knew that he'd keep a lower profile if he didn't wear his *Bryce Academy* ring in public, but that was the one thing he refused to give up. It might be the past, but it was his past.

Djamila had even talked him into wearing mufti tonight, which just felt wrong. But for her, he would.

Corduroy slacks in a shade that split the difference between maroon and indigo. Dress tunic in a salmon that shouldn't have worked, but did. He'd have never made that decision, certainly, but Adrian Ahmad, one of the stevedores who handled cargo, was also something of a fashion expert, and had assured him that he could pull it off.

So he'd let Djamila take him out on a date. Onto the station, even. In public. Dressed like this.

He felt like a rooster strutting onto a stage.

Didn't help that Adrian had apparently also done a number for Djamila. On Djamila.

Zakhar's jaw had dropped, the first time he saw it. She'd blushed to the tips of her ears and down as low as the front of what that dress showed, which was far more than usual for his dragoon.

Dove gray. Silk looking, but that didn't mean anything with the fabric printers that they had aboard *Excalibur*. From the strings tying things, you started on one hip, wrapping around her muscular bottom to the other hip, then across her belly and up at an angle that captured one breast but not the other. Under the arm, then up and across her shoulders, leaving a slash of flesh across her shoulder blades. Down across the front of her left shoulder and back to the starting point, tied in front with just enough knot that it wouldn't accidentally come undone over dinner, or if they went dancing later.

Still, it would be like peeling an orange to get her out of it. Probably even more fun, too.

Her eyes held that promise as the waiter removed plates and deposited dessert menus before refilling coffee.

Zakhar was off duty, but the pirate he'd been for so long was never far from the surface.

Couple across the room were eyeing him in ways that didn't rise to the level of unleashing the Ballerina of Death, as Javier still teasingly called Djamila occasionally.

Not yet.

Man and woman. Late twenties from the feel. Dressed modestly and boring, in dark gray for him and darker blue for her. Looked like Anglos, but Zakhar wouldn't hold that against them.

He'd rapped his ring on the table top at one point. Old habit. The woman's head had come around sharply and she'd said something to the man. Both had leaned in and whispered.

Nothing more. No sudden comm calls that might bring gendarmes or bounty hunters running. Heavens knew Zakhar had both chasing him for various things accumulated over the decades of being a small-scale pirate warlord.

The old days.

At the same time, those two kept watch like hawks. And it felt to him like it was that damnable ring that had gotten them excited in the first place.

Bryce Academy. Class of 549. Shit, was he really going to be celebrating forty years soon? Twenty years active duty with the *Concord* Navy. Nineteen as a…call it a civilian. Close enough for government work. Pirate. Retired pirate. Explorer today, commanding a First-Rate Galleon while that dangerous goofball known as *The Science Officer* worked his impossible charm and magic on people across the galaxy.

Good thing Javier was back on the ship tonight. You never knew when you might need stupid amounts of firepower and crazy people to break you out of jail.

Not that he had any experience with that sort of thing, Your Honor. Lucky bystander and all that.

But those two were in his head. Under his fingernail like a splinter.

"Should I have kept the steak knife when they took our plates?" Djamila asked quietly.

Her eyes were locked on his, but that was her way of tracking the entire room behind her, because she knew where he was staring. And if he reacted, she'd uncoil like a venomous snake.

Two hundred and ten centimeters of deadly. Brown hair buzzed short on the sides for a spacesuit helmet and spiked on top. It was starting to come in gray now, elegant silver threads.

He was bald enough to keep everything but a gray Van Dyke shaved so he didn't have to admit he wasn't thirty anymore.

But Djamila would be forty this year. They were all getting older, even that silly Peter Pan, Javier.

"No," he said, after weighing the odds.

Unless the pair over there had guns and were trained killers, Djamila could take them. By herself. That wrap was hung in such a way that she had freedom to move if she wanted, even with it asymmetrically hanging past one knee.

"Which table?" she asked.

"First right past the front desk," Zakhar said.

"Younger couple," Djamila nodded. "Here when we came in. Lingering over dinner still?"

"Watching us," he nodded. "Me. And I have the impression they're watching my ring more than us."

"Interesting," she replied.

Like a light switch had been flipped, the Dragoon replaced his date. Stunning and beautiful still, but the slinkiness she'd been practicing earlier was gone, replaced with a hardness that would hold a razor tip even as you chipped marble with it.

"Are they doing anything?" Djamila inquired.

"Watching," Zakhar said. "Nothing more."

"Ring marks you," she said with a sly grin. "*Concord* Naval Officer and all that noise."

"We are a long ways from the *Concord*," Zakhar reminded her. "No idea why someone might want to bother me. Maybe they recognized *Excalibur* and put two and two together?"

She shrugged in a way that caused his heart to skip a beat, stretching and pulling her shoulders back. Not much chest on the woman, but lots of muscles. She still did handstand pushups against a wall every morning. If she spent the night in his cabin, she'd even do them nude so he could watch and ogle.

Lots to ogle. All of it wonderful.

"Should we skip dessert and force the situation now, or drag it out and see if they have the patience?" she asked.

Tactical. Combat-oriented killer. One of the best he'd ever known at it.

And an amazing woman on top of all that.

"Tempted to walk right over and sit down with them," Zakhar said. "Can't think of a culture where staring at someone so openly over dinner isn't rude bordering on insulting. Also thinking about getting them into a station corridor for the confrontation. Thoughts?"

"Outside," she said. "Easier to control things, and I'd hate to get blacklisted from this restaurant. We might never make it back this way, but we might, and that ribeye was amazing."

"Agreed," Zakhar nodded. It had been.

He turned down the offer of dessert and settled up the bill. Plus, they had a French bistro on the ship that loved to experiment with pastries and sweets, buying random cookbooks on every planet the ship had traveled to in order to find more things to try.

He could get something later.

Zakhar rose at the same time Djamila did, and made his way to the door behind her, walking right past the couple who'd been watching him.

PART 2

Djamila had been hard-pressed to wear such an outfit in public, but Adrian had convinced her that it would work. Having watched so many people stare at her thighs and chest tonight, she believed. And felt three meters tall.

She had almost as much mobility as if she were nude, the way he'd designed and sewn it. Not that she'd do that short of a mission.

An important mission.

But she'd grown more comfortable with herself, just as she and Zakhar had with each other. Javier's fault, though she'd never tell him that. Afia Burakgazi had also contributed. Even Suvi.

The crew was more of a family these days than any place she'd ever lived, including home in *Neu Berne* before she'd joined the fleet.

All of that, however, was another layer of cloth that would slip off as easily as this dress Adrian had made for her.

She stared at the two who had gotten Zakhar's attention,

pacing slowly in his wake to the door in order to see what they did. Anglo pale skin with fine brown hair on both of them. Younger than her by at least a decade. Neither had the shape or structure of someone who had undergone military service. That got into the spine and never left.

Even today, Djamila had to work at not looking like a soldier.

Dressing like a beautiful woman helped. Or had.

She walked like a killing machine right now, measuring strides towards that table and placing things like empty chairs and bottles that could turn into weapons in an eye-blink.

Zakhar surprised her some by slowing as he approached the table. Didn't speak. Didn't stop. Merely turned his head sufficient that he was also staring at them, then he continued before either of them got the courage to speak.

Djamila had also slowed. Lagged a full stride behind in case one of them did something stupid. Then Zakhar was out the hatch and out of sight. She went after him, though she only made it two steps to where he'd turned and slipped his back to the bulkhead, nearly invisible behind a fern at first glance.

He caught her hand and pulled her next to him. In any other scenario, it might be for a quick smooch. IN PUBLIC EVEN. But not tonight.

They watched like hawks. A few moments later, the couple emerged, looking around almost panicky, until they saw her eyes over the fern plant and a hint of fear came into the man's eyes.

Gotcha.

She only smiled, though. Zakhar wanted to get them out in the main station corridor. It was geo-synched to the planet *Ninovskaya*, with the planetary capital more or less straight down. Late in the planetary day, but stations ran around the clock, just like warships.

Still, traffic was thin currently. Station security would be meandering around, mostly to be seen, rather than as a threat. Nobody caused trouble on stations.

At least not in places like *Ninovskaya*.

Still, Djamila was prepared to cause trouble. Not looking forward to it, heavens forbid.

Prepared. That was all.

The two Anglos paled under her gaze. She nodded them closer. Might as well have this out now.

They approached, looking more like kittens than tigers. She fought to keep her smile friendly enough.

Any sudden movements for a weapon and they'd be on their backs. Dead or unconscious would be a split-second decision when they forced her.

"Your pardon," the male said hesitantly. "Are you Captain Sokolov?"

Zakhar was on her far side, where they had to talk past her. Get past her, if they wanted to get stupid. Djamila preferred it that way.

"I am," he said simply. "Did you have business with *Excalibur*? My on-station agent is handling both cargo and passengers. You can reach her in the morning."

He stood still, so Djamila did as well. They didn't look like travelers interested in booking passage on a ship like *Excalibur*. And weren't dressed nearly well enough to be shippers.

"It is not that, Captain," the man said, taking another tentative half step closer.

Probably didn't realize that he was already close enough that she could get to him with a single step. Djamila watched and listened.

Predator.

"What he is trying to say, Captain," the woman spoke now, "is that we would like to inquire about hiring your ship."

"Hiring?"

Zakhar packed an amazing amount of disdain into such a small word. He was good with language that way.

"We have a problem, Captain Sokolov," the woman nodded. "Pirates. Nobody else will help us, so we have come to *Ninovskaya* seeking assistance."

"Pirates?" he inquired.

She could tell by the tone of his voice that the *Concord* officer she'd first fallen in love with had suddenly awakened from the calm man who had been her date tonight.

"Locusts, Captain," the male said. "They descend on us and strip our farms and villages bare, leaving us barely enough food and livestock to survive so they can come back again the following year."

Djamila glanced back, but already knew what she'd see. He was standing taller, not that he'd been slumped at any point.

Harder.

The *Concord* saw itself as the good guys across a wide swath of the galaxy. After *Neu Berne* had lost the Great War to the *Union of Man* and *Balustrade*, they'd largely inherited hegemony, having as big a fleet as everyone else put together at that point.

Djamila still remembered the lean years in her youth, after reparations had stripped things bare in a manner one might also describe as locusts.

At the same time, *Neu Berne* had started it, so the others had been intent on crushing her homeland's ability and willingness to fight future wars.

Even after so long, Zakhar wore his class ring from the *Bryce Academy* in public, the sort of thing that other *Bryce* graduates saw and recognized.

Javier had been another one like Zakhar. Once they'd taken that man prisoner, he'd worked his magic on the crew, and turned them from poor pirates into...something.

It was too much to suggest heroes, but Djamila wondered how history might regard the man, if the truth ever got out. Already, there were whispers of *The Science Officer* out there. If she was only a cast member in his legend, that was still more than she'd deserved or expected out of her career or life.

"Pirates," Zakhar repeated, but this time it wasn't a question.

Excalibur was a warship. A First-Rate Galleon refurbished bow to stern by the Khatum of *Altai* for this voyage. As good as anything up to and including a Class II Warmaster. They were starting to build things categorized as Class III now, but only a few. And only places like the *Concord*.

Suvi and *Excalibur* were more than capable of handling pirates.

And Djamila could tell Zakhar was intrigued. Javier probably would be as well.

If she was ambivalent, that was an understanding that trouble always found those two men, and she'd be there to shoot it dead.

She was good at that.

"This is not the place to have such a discussion," Zakhar said after a moment. "Give me your card and we will make arrangements to bring you aboard our ship tomorrow."

The woman ended up having that information. Djamila took it from her, then watched them scurry quickly away.

She studied Zakhar's face once they were alone again.

"Smells like a trap," he said simply.

Djamila nodded. She'd had that same question. *Too good to be true* usually was.

"And bringing them aboard the ship?" she pressed as they started walking again.

"I control the battlefield at that point," he smiled up at her. "Or rather, you and Suvi do, which is even better, as far as I'm concerned."

"Now what?" she asked.

"Now?" he grinned. "Now, I have the rest of the evening to have you to myself. I have been looking forward to that."

She smiled.

So had she.

PART 3

Javier wasn't nearly as enamored of righteous causes and heroic legends as *some of the crew*, names at present left to the thinly-veiled imagination. Sort of like that stripper's veil that covered exactly enough to legally be a thing.

Still, he'd hired Zakhar for this gig. Djamila represented the ship's Centurions. Afia was Shop Steward for the rest of the crew. Javier had multiple shares as technical owner of the vessel itself, standing in for the woman appearing on a screen next to Afia.

Suvi was the ship. His goofball daughter who composed symphonies and told dirty jokes, but she was also armed to the teeth with a *Neu Berne* battleship he'd stolen. With a little help from the rest of his friends.

Best thing around to smash pirates, with the old *Concord* Strike Corvette *Storm Gauntlet* so badly damaged that melting the parts down had been a better investment of time.

This afternoon, he was in the forward lounge with Zakhar's two stray ducks. Bethany, Mary-Elizabeth, and Piet were there as well, since they were serving officers, but

Djamila would exercise their vote if it came down to an argument over such things.

The man was Cornell Hawthorne, about as English a name as Javier thought he'd ever heard. But then, *Byormi* had mostly been settled by English stock drawn originally from their little island on the homeworld, back when regions were still occasionally grouped into nations.

The woman was Nita Reeves. If Cornell had sandy-brown hair, hers was just brown. Dull and lusterless. Fine, but not anything she took pride in or care of. Same could be said for the pair of them. Thin but dull folks. Not unattractive, but nothing about them stood out and demanded your attention.

Even in speaking, they were dull. Fortunately, Javier had taken one look at them when Zakhar brought them aboard, and done himself a triple shot espresso with some caramel syrup. Probably end up paying for it later, but at least he was still awake, even as some of the others were being badly hypnotized by Cornell's droning voice.

"Let's stop right there," Javier broke into the monotonous description.

Everyone suddenly perked up some as newness disrupted the impending nap.

"Sir?" Cornell asked, also seeming to awaken himself.

"You call them *The Horde*," Javier explained. "Right? Mob of small Jump-capable ships that look like they all came out of a junkyard, rather than a squadron of identical craft? Swoop down in their multitudes, shooting anything they want and stealing everything that catches their eye? How many of these little ships are we talking?"

It appeared to be a force of effort to get the man out of the mental rut he'd stumbled into, but eventually he turned to Nita for confirmation.

She struck Javier as the smarter of the two. But a lot of worlds and cultures in this slice of the galaxy seemed to be stuck in a chauvinistic mindset where women were second-class.

Dumbasses, but nobody had made him Emperor of the Universe to fix it. Nobody smart would.

"Scores," Nita said now. "Sometimes hundreds."

"Each of them ranging from maybe a crew of a handful up to a cutter with maybe twenty or thirty?" he pressed, seeing the shape of it in his head.

He'd never scouted this sector, back when it was just him and Suvi, but history and culture tended to rhyme more often than most people really understood, unless they were smart and hired themselves a hot genius librarian like Bethany to handle those research tasks.

"And each of those ships probably mounts a pulsar forward," Javier continued. "Fixed centerline mount. Maybe stubby wings if they have two of them. You gotta be one of the bigger ones to put it in a turret, because the lines are different. And I'll bet the biggest one mounts a Pulse Cannon. Although, if they are really pirates, it'll be an Ion Cannon instead. Easier to capture something you want to steal and strip if you don't blow it up in the process."

Javier glanced over at Zakhar fast enough to catch the grimace in the man's eyes. *Storm Gauntlet* had done it that way, including the time they had captured him.

Old pirate tricks were old because they worked.

"Yes, that describes them as well as anything," Nita said, still not getting it.

But then, civilians rarely got it. You had to be a trained, *professional* sailor to understand some of those things.

"Won't work," Javier said simply.

Might as well puncture that balloon of pomposity now, rather than sidling up to it later.

Zakhar started to surge to his feet faster than his brain caught up with his heart or his ego. But he caught himself. Grimaced so deep it looked like it hurt, then leaned back.

Everyone had turned to him anyway, so he shrugged.

"He's right," Zakhar said.

At least such an admission didn't look like it physically pained the man as much as it might have five or six years ago.

And Zakhar's admission set off a babble of arguments and noise ranging back and forth across the room.

Javier let it go for a bit, so folks would at least get it out of their systems, then he turned to Suvi's screen and made a quick gesture that went back to the old days.

She blipped the alert siren for about a quarter of a second. Barely enough to matter, but almost everyone here had lived under military discipline for years.

They all fell silent. Most of them were half-standing before their minds caught up.

"*Excalibur* has twelve-centimeter pulsars on every facing," Javier explained to the newcomers. "They're getting smaller with technology and time, so we refitted a few of them with six-centimeter pulse cannons. Got a whole series of torpedo tubes fore and aft, any one of which would blow a cutter hull to hell and gone easily. That's not the problem."

Even Suvi finally caught on, but she'd been like Zakhar, reacting with her *Concord* training that demanded she rush into a burning building like a firefighter.

"Suvi, assume a swarm of two hundred such craft as Cornell has described," he instructed her, watching everyone turn to her screen. "Assume pilots not as good as Del, but competent enough to make a living at this sort of shenanigans."

She thought at something like thirty thousand times the speed of a human in her newest hardware, so reactions on her face were there for his benefit. Or rather, everyone else. In the space of a heartbeat, she could change outfits several times, write a symphony, and read several volumes of history or biographies. Plus watch a few movies.

Her face fell.

"Shit," she muttered, mostly under her breath.

The best part? He'd turned her into a person. No other Sentience he'd ever met was capable of swearing, let alone writing music.

His legacy, because she'd outlive him by a long stretch, if they were both careful.

"Suvi?" Zakhar asked.

"I might pull it off," she said, her own tones gone dark. "If I was lucky and they were stupid. At the same time, my scenarios lean heavily towards this ship suffering significant, and possibly catastrophic, damage in the process."

"She was designed by *Neu Berne* to engage other warships of her class," Javier told the two strangers. "Back when she was the flagship of their fleet during the Great War. Nobody built locust tactics in those days. Still don't really. That is a pirate thing."

"So there's nothing you can do?" Cornell asked, deflating as Javier watched.

"Nothing *we* can do," Javier grinned at the man.

Djamila, of all people, saw it first. Her eyes got huge, then laughing, then utterly devious, all in the blink of an eye. Just one of the reasons he loved her. Or whatever.

"No?" Nita asked.

"No," Javier assured her. "But I know a guy that might be able to help."

"Oh?" She looked like someone had tossed her lifesuits in a hull breach. Cornell was the same. "Who?"

"Captain Eutropio Navarre," Javier said.

PART 4

Bethany hadn't been there in the so-called Navarre Days, so everything she knew came from after-action reports and stories she had accumulated from interviewing the crew. All written down, but not shared outside the hull. Statutes of Limitations, and all that.

Maybe fifty years after everybody was dead, Suvi could see to it that the locks on those records were opened for scholars and disbelievers to learn some of the truth about her boss.

Captain Sokolov was not her commanding officer, weird as that was. The ship was an entirely civilian affair, and she'd been hired by the owners. Javier and the Khatum of *Altai*, Behnam Sherazi. Not Javier's spouse. She would never get married and already had grown children, one of whom would inherit the planet, the power, the wealth, and the position one of these days.

Still, the other half of the thing that made Javier whole. Bethany knew him well enough now to understand that.

Hadn't slept with the man, though many of the crew did without any jealousy. Might yet, one of these days.

Today, she felt like the good angel on his right shoulder, arguing with the devil on the left.

They'd talked Cornell and Nita empty, then sent them back to the station in order to have a private chat.

Same group as before. The Inner Circle of folks that Javier listened to. That included her, because she'd been hired to find the man precedent and information.

As he'd said just now: History didn't repeat, but it often rhymed. She supposed that made her something of a musicologist, if you wanted to look at it that way.

"We need intelligence," she said as everyone settled, this time largely shifting away from caffeine to alcohol. She'd even poured herself a little wine. "I can get you all sorts of answers, but you have to let me ask questions first."

"Understood," Javier replied with a sharp nod. "The one place we can't go is *Byormi*."

"Why not?" Bethany asked, looking around the nods.

But then, these folks were all pirates. Former pirates, she amended herself.

"Because we lose the element of surprise," Zakhar noted. "Right now, those pirates would have no idea that the locals they've been preying on might have finally had enough. Might finally be ready to fight back. Wouldn't do settlers any good to buy guns, because they wouldn't know how to use them. They need to buy gunners. Or rent them, in this case."

"But Suvi believes that *Excalibur* can't take on that mob," Bethany replied, uncertain where this was going.

"And she is probably correct," Zakhar said. "Two hundred is probably the high-end, worst-case scenario, but not out of line. And likely what they could lay hands on if *Byormi* suddenly thought that a warship could protect them."

"Okay?" Bethany was confused.

Not an unusual circumstance with this group.

"Javier, you going to pull a fast one on the pirate base?" Afia asked.

All eyes turned to the man who might be known to certain folks as Navarre.

"I have no idea," the man replied cheerfully. "That's where Bethany and some of the rest of you come into play. These folks operate on a world somewhere within reasonable flight time to *Byormi*. Probably at the center of a whole ring of such targets. Farming worlds and new colonies that they can attack because none of them have the money to do something about it."

"But you think that *Byormi* does?" Djamila asked.

Javier laughed.

"Hell, no," he said. "If anything, they're probably utterly broke and hoping that a sob story and maybe a few tons of grain would entice us to go be heroes."

"But we're going to do it anyway?" the tall woman pressed.

Javier sobered. Bethany was getting used to the mercurial shifts of personality that the man evinced on a regular basis. Larger than life in many ways, but under it all was a calm certainty that she'd rarely known in anyone.

"When we were done with *Kimmeria*, and all those folks, we had a conversation," he reminded her in a tone just a shade shy of deadly. "Bethany here asked if we were out to save the galaxy. Remember that?"

Heads nodded, including hers. She'd signed on for what she'd expected to be piracy with a fancier title, and instead had become a knight errant under King Javier. Or something equally silly and serious.

"That means things like this," Javier continued. "Doing right because nobody else can. Because it is the right thing to do, if we want to somehow blunt or limit that rising storm that Dorn assures me is coming in my lifetime, assuming I die of old age back on *Altai*. Because bad people exist, and *must be stopped*."

"Simple as that?" Bethany asked, astonished at the scope of what he was implying about their grand voyage, all the way from *Altai*, though they were on their way home finally. Maybe.

Javier straightened his shoulders, and she saw the admiral he might have become, had life and loss not intruded. He might have been doing this from the deck of a proper *Concord* Warmaster, at the head of a full fleet.

Except that he wouldn't.

The *Concord* saw peace on all sides, with all their ancient foes weak. They were cutting back defense spending and relaxing their vigilance. *Byormi* was too far away to bother with, even at the peak of the *Concord*'s power, and they had slid off that peak about the time Bethany had first been commissioned.

Slowly, sure, but certainly. Down.

Bandits and pirate kings were the kinds of folks to fill in the gaps that emerged.

And wandering heroes like Javier.

"Yes," Javier answered her question. "Simple as that."

"How?"

Then he smiled, and the joker was back.

"Kid, I got no clue," he laughed. "You and Afia will be in charge of whatever research you need to do to figure that out. Me, Djamila, and Zakhar cannot be visible at any time. *Excalibur* may have to change transponder signals to pretend to be some other ship, though not many people will be fooled. At the same time, pirates won't have a sophisticated intelligence-gathering operation to see what we're up to, so Captain Navarre can come and go."

"And it is all going to be a con game, correct?" Bethany asked.

Javier had never struck her as having any sort of death

wish. Nor being the kind of adrenaline junkie who would get in over his head.

No, he and Zakhar, and the others, seemed utterly convinced that they could do this thing.

Javier nodded.

Calm certainty.

She wasn't sure she understood, but she didn't need to.

Her job was to get Javier information he could use to pull it off.

Then write it all down later for future historians to boggle at.

Because they would.

VALADRIS

PART 1

Afia looked around the crowd as she and Bethany exited the starport terminal. She'd never been to *Valadris*, but after a while you develop a sixth sense for such places. Helped that her grandmother was a witch and had hexed her early on with the Second Sight. Or something.

Kept her out of trouble, for the most part. Useful when you were only one hundred and fifty centimeters tall and skinny. Bethany was like a tree standing next to her. The only thing worse would have been bringing the Dragoon. Afia sometimes felt like an eight-year-old, walking around next to Djamila Sykora.

Valadris, on the other hand, had a population of folks dark enough that Afia fit in better than Bethany, which was nice. She was Anglo-Indonesian and had grown up in the Yukon Protectorate, back on Earth. Folks around her had that same black hair and golden-brown skin that made the tall librarian stand out.

Afia might use that offensively later. Get those pretty, blue eyes batting at someone. Then tell them she was a historian.

The right people would be all hot and bothered at that point and Afia could pick their brains.

Shame Javier wasn't along, but that just meant this was a girl's weekend, out causing trouble.

Not that Bethany did that sort of thing, but she was slowly loosening up from the stick-up-her-butt naval officer Javier had first hired. Turning into a proper pirate babe.

Afia smiled at the entire world and walked. A cute girl across the way blinked at her and smiled back, but Afia wasn't ready to seduce any locals yet. Just happy to be on the ground, enjoying planetary weather.

Helped that the day was cool and drizzly. Like home. Barely twelve degrees out, and just enough wet floating in it that your hair went flat. Hers was short right now. Too much time in space suits to want to braid it all the time.

Pixie, in all the good ways.

She nodded up to Bethany and turned left. Just because Grandma's Second Sight told her to. Skipped the line of taxis hauling folks greater distances than they could walk. Instead, over to the tram station and catch the rail into town. They had reservations for two rooms at a nicer hotel not far from the big university on planet.

Would have been nice to bring *Dr. Javier Aritza of King's College* down to bamboozle folks. Look at what he'd done to those silly academics on *Ormint*, seducing the Drs. Askvig into helping them discover tree 'roos.

Afia laughed out of sheer joy and grinned up at Bethany's arch look of semi-confusion.

"Yer nuts," the librarian muttered with a quick grin and a shake of her head.

"And?" Afia laughed again.

Felt good to be alive. To be doing something good. Too many years as a pirate handing out evil to folks. She didn't figure they'd balance out those scales anytime soon, but that wasn't the same as not working to fix her overall karma.

"So what's the plan?" Bethany asked. "You look like you have one."

"Nope." Afia couldn't contain the grins, so she didn't try. "Gonna get to the hotel and make sure our luggage got delivered. Maybe eat. Then score some nightlife."

"Not hit the university library?" Bethany asked next, maybe a little put out.

"Oh, babe," Afia said. "What I need to know won't be written down anywhere but wanted posters."

She'd checked, and they were largely alone on the platform right now, so speaking was fine. Couple of cute boys watching from the distance, but they looked like office drones, rather than criminal elements she might need to...*question*.

"I see," Bethany said.

Maybe she did. Afia doubted it, though. Girl had spent her life in stacks, taking orders from captains and admirals.

Afia had had a...*much more colorful decade.*

"So I should pack my stunner?" Bethany asked in a quieter tone. "As well as a spare shirt?"

"Always," Afia nodded. "Places we need to go are a little rougher. I'd have brought the Dragoon if that was an option, but she's going to be on stage later, so she and Navarre have to appear at the same time, and he's not ready for that."

The train arrived about then and Afia lapsed into silence.

Not a lot of folks riding with them when it got moving again, and she'd walked them to the far end of the platform, so they were in the last car. Plus, she put a growl on her face when folks looked her way.

They were alone.

"Tell me about Hadiiye," Bethany said quietly as they started into town.

"Wilhelmina Teague, originally," Afia nodded. "We rescued her from the place Javier calls the *Mind Field* in a deliberate misspelling. When the Dragoon got captured, 'Mina and Javier created two characters to infiltrate the warship *Salekhard* and Abraam Tamaz, our old First Officer, but he was slightly before my time."

Afia noted that Bethany was focused. Probably memorizing things, or recording it on her pocket comm for later. All going into a book at some point. Or a whole series of them.

Immortality, at least of a sort. At the same time, if Afia was going to tell these stories, she had a duty to do it right.

"Captain Navarre is all the bad parts of Javier," she continued. "Hadiiye was his gun-moll, killer babe sidekick. 'Mina is about your height. Maybe a little taller. Plus boots. Taught women martial arts five centuries ago, and had several blackbelts in a variety of things, so she could pull it off."

"And Navarre?" Bethany asked.

Afia considered her words carefully. She shared Javier with several other folks, all of whom knew that they were second-string to the Khatum herself. But that was okay. Behnam was one hell of a woman.

"Navarre will frighten the shit out of you when you finally meet him," Afia said. "He frightens me. Still. And I know the truth. Javier taps into that dark place that broke his original career with the *Concord* Navy. All the grief. All the rage. All the bad stuff. Carries it like armor. Exudes it like a perfume. You'll be attracted to it, and repelled. Enthralled and disgusted. Wet and frightened."

Bethany nodded her head in a tiny motion, like it might fall off if she moved too far. Part of that was never taking Javier to bed. Man was amazing when you had his attention. Attentive. Reciprocative. Mind-blowing.

That let Afia see past the various shells he carried around even today. The joker, the goofball, the cook, the nerd, the botanist.

And the killer.

"But he's always there underneath," Afia continued. "Always Javier. After *Salekhard*, they went to *Shangdu* and killed a man by breaking into the Khatum's vaults and stealing all the documentation indicating that the guy was the rightful king. The hidden and previously overthrown heir to the Jianwen Empire. Never touched a hair on his head. Snuck out safely. He'd already seduced the Khatum. Or her him. That delicacy convinced her that he wasn't an enemy. Then later, Walvisbaai pissed him and Zakhar off, so Navarre had to come back and create an incident so extravagant that nobody would ever bother him again."

"Until now," Bethany said.

Afia nodded.

"That man hates bullies," she said, as if that summed it all up.

In a way, it did. The Dragoon had been a bully when they'd met, so she'd beat him up a few times. Then he'd gone and saved her life because, as he'd put it, nobody got to kill her but him. And vice versa.

Now, the two of them, Navarre and Hadiiye, were coming back.

Afia would have felt bad for the pirates, but she was pretty sure they had it coming.

Everybody had it coming eventually.

PART 2

Bethany had taken Afia's advice and dressed dark and sedate. They didn't want to look like a pair of party girls out for a good time where they were going, so she was in dark pants tough enough for engineering duty, plus a couple of layers of shirts and a jacket. Pockets filled with cash, comm, and two stunners, because if she needed one, she wanted it handy, whichever pocket she reached for.

The door of the place Afia had found—how had she known about this place if she'd never been to *Valadris* before? —was guarded by a couple of guys who might be Djamila Sykora's cousins, based on their height and mass. Bethany was hard-pressed to believe that they were human, as big and wide as they were.

Friendly, though. Afia had walked down the steps to this underground joint, right up to the men, and charmed them. Rather like Javier could do.

They hadn't even charged a cover to let the two of them in.

Place was dim on the verge of dark when they got

through the doors. Loud on the edge of painful, with a live band playing up on a stage at the far end of the space. Nothing like Suvi composed, but Bethany reached into her pocket and flipped the recorder on, because the woman would want samples later. Might be listening now, but Bethany wasn't sure how good a signal she had down here under the building without pulling out the device and checking.

Sausage fest kind of place. Men outnumbered women about two or three to one, which explained the no cover charge part. Hard crowd, too. The sort of place where officers like her didn't usually go, but knew where to look when sailors went missing. Possibly passed out drunk in a booth or back alley nearby.

Rough.

Afia surfed the crowds like a pro. Bethany slid along in her wake.

To the bar, the tiny woman ordered two bottles of something, got horribly overcharged back even on *Bryce*, and left a tip and a smile as she moved on to a booth up on one side.

Bethany watched Afia open each bottle with care, confirming the seals were intact. Easy enough to drop something in a woman's cup when she was distracted.

At least Afia had arranged for the Dragoon to supply backup.

Looking around, she noted Sascha Koç and Hajna Flores seated at another table not far away, with Iqbal Kader and Helmfried Arif. Djamila's two pathfinders, with two of the men Javier always referred to as *Gunbunnies*, though these days it was a term of respect instead of the old derision she'd heard about.

All four were deadly in a league perhaps one relegation down from Djamila, but far above Bethany and Afia. They were not, however, officers or intellectuals. Afia might only be a shop steward by her admission, but she was generally recognized on the ship as First Assistant Engineer.

Andreea Dalca, the Chief Engineer, was about as introverted as you could get and still be functional. Hardly ever left her space of engineering, cafeteria, and her quarters. That put Afia as the face of the organization aft.

Men wandered by as they sat and sipped, listening to the music. The noise was not to Bethany's tastes, but seemed to be entertaining the crowd, from the mob on the dance floor and the number of tables and booths full.

Afia scowled at all of the folks circling like sharks, until one came along and made a complicated hand gesture that Bethany didn't fully understand. Afia replied with something similar, like two folks conversing in sign language. They went back and forth for a time, then the man walked away.

"What just happened?" Bethany leaned over to her co-conspirator and asked.

"He's not the guy I'm looking for, but he has a cousin," Afia said with a hard grin. "They always have a cousin. Anyway, the cousin might be the right guy, but he has to go find him. We're hanging out for a bit."

"Okay, sure," Bethany said, utterly lost.

Still, Afia seemed confident. And the two pathfinders and dates were handy if there was trouble, studiously ignoring things right now like strangers.

She drank and waited. Librarians were experts at patience. Military librarians had to deal with clueless admirals, so they also knew how to keep a perfectly innocent face at all times.

She had not expected that skill to figure so prominently as a pirate. Or maybe she had.

A woman approached. As before, hand signals back and forth formed a conversation Bethany was excluded from.

She focused on the woman's face instead.

Dyed black hair at odds with the vast wastelands of canyons and wrinkles that made up her face. Sharp eyes that looked black. Liver spots on her hands and slack skin on her neck.

Old, but utterly vibrant. Sharp, laughing eyes as she slid into the booth directly across from Bethany and signaled to someone nearby. A man put a glass down in front of her then withdrew. Unfortunate when he did, because he ended up standing about a meter away with his back to Sascha and Helmfried if trouble broke out.

Unfortunate for him, anyway.

"You come looking for information?" the old woman finally asked, voice barely audible with the music jamming so loudly around them.

"Broker," Afia said. "Been hired by someone to get him in contact with the Pirates of *Syntha*."

That got a sharp look out of the woman.

"Who?" she demanded sharply.

"Captain Eutropio Navarre," Afia replied. "Man's shifting his field of operations from the east to closer sectors. *Concord*'s hot and bothered to arrest him for shit, so he wants out of their reach. Before he sets up shop here, he wanted to work some understandings and deals with local competitors."

"Navarre is coming here?" the woman asked, eyes showing a little more white than they had before.

The first edge of nervous fear creeping in.

"He's already here," Afia laughed in a cruel, cutting way that was absolutely nothing like the woman Bethany knew. "He's trying to keep a low profile for a bit, so he hired my organization to scout. *Syntha* seems to be a name folks are bandying around, but they aren't anybody we know. They a problem? Will they be a problem if Navarre starts working these sectors? Will they object and need to be crushed like bugs?"

Bethany let her face fall into a scowl and watched the woman. She was here as a sidekick to a fixer, or whatever role

Afia was playing. All a scam, but that described most of what Javier had planned, with the input of everyone.

Navarre could bring death and destruction. And he could swindle you blind. Pick your poison?

"They run a loose ship," the old woman said in reply, speaking carefully. "Less an organization than a culture. Folks occasionally refer to them accurately as a horde. Trouble, but not an army. Dangerous, but unfocused until someone pisses them off. Then the whole mob gathers up like one of their raids."

"How organized is *Syntha* itself?" Bethany asked.

She'd done some research, but there wasn't much available. Didn't help that *Valadris* was almost the opposite corner of the sector from *Syntha* and the worlds they raided.

The old woman studied her. Bethany concentrated on looking like a librarian. Useful guise. Accurate enough, too. Afia's supposed organization would need folks like her as much as they needed smooth talkers like Afia.

"I'm not sure they can spell organized," the woman finally said. "Woman in charge right now is Zhenya Kovalev. At least last time I checked. She allows towns and villages to have local governments, as long as nobody tries to grab anything bigger than about a county. She doesn't own the planet or run it, but nobody challenges her. If Navarre is going to work with her, he'll also have to deal with her witchdoctor. Fellow named Orlov. Not an assistant. Not a psychologist. Pirate first and foremost. Dangerous man. Almost as dangerous as Mila Vinogradov, who is completely insane. Why's Navarre coming here?"

Bethany nodded towards Afia. She had no idea what lies and stories the woman was spinning, or had worked out with Javier, so she could keep quiet on that sort of thing. Her job was to understand the political and social ramifications contained in those few sentences, and prep Javier and Djamila for what was coming.

If anyone could.

PART 3

Afia was mostly making this shit up as she went. Nothing she told the old crone would matter at the end of the day, because Navarre and *Excalibur* wouldn't actually stay around long. They had a dinner date with the Khatum, back on *Altai*.

Not so close that they had to rush, but not far enough out that they could dawdle anywhere. Or fall back into piracy as anything but a cover story.

And hitting pirates for fun served a lot of benefits across a wide space.

"The reason Navarre is coming this way is that the *Concord* Navy is still pissed about what he did at *Nidavellir*," Afia said. "Man blew up an orbital platform and crushed a chunk of another pirate clan's fleet in the process. Rained pieces down on the planet below. Kinda rude, even if they deserved it. And *Nidavellir* and Walvisbaai did. For now, he's been keeping a low profile. Smaller jobs. Political assassinations. Governments destabilized. Nothing big enough to draw in the *Concord* or anybody over here. None of them worry him. It's the professional courtesy with the folks at *Syntha* that we're here to cover."

She nodded to include Bethany in that. The two of them represented a shadowy new organization Afia was inventing from whole cloth to school these folks on how to run a good con. Plus, she had a warship backing her up, and a stupid amount of armed troopers willing to shoot first.

Made a girl feel a little feisty. And more than one person called her a *Pixie Kodiak*.

"Nobody can speak for *Syntha* but Kovalev herself," the woman said.

"Understood," Afia nodded. "We're trying to smooth things so that Navarre can go in there and have a polite chat with the woman, rather than having to hit orbit and start blasting things because folks got no manners."

She watched the woman's eyes get a little big and fearful. At the same time, Javier, Zakhar, and Suvi had gone to *Nidavellir* and done bad shit. She'd been involved, right up to the point that a chunk of that shuttle's hull went through her belly left of center. Would've killed her, but for Ilan suddenly turning into a grownup.

Any resemblance to the clumsy man she'd first met when she came aboard was entirely accidental at this point. He wasn't into the combat engineering side of things as much as her, but might still end up taking Andreea's spot as Chief Engineer when that woman retired one of these days.

Afia enjoyed going off and having adventures too much to be chained to a desk. Andreea had that covered. Then someone else would do paperwork.

"He has a warship?" the crone asked.

Afia laughed loud enough that heads turned.

"Yeah," she said, leaving it at that.

Folks starting shit with Suvi were tired of living, obviously. She might not be able to take on a pirate raid head on when they were a plague of locusts, but if you fed them at her randomly, she could kill hundreds of little ships before you took her down.

Assuming you could, even then.

"You staying around here?" the crone asked.

"For a few days," Afia replied. "Checking the local scene to see if we want to open a branch office on *Valadris*. Navarre's ship and crew are also capable of hauling cargo and people, but the freightage costs are high. Keeps out the riffraff."

The crone reached into a pocket of her top and pulled out a card, handing it to Afia.

"Contact me there tomorrow," she said. "I'll put out a few messages and see what connections wish to make Navarre's acquaintance while he's around. I suspect that there will only be a few, if he's being chased by lightning."

"Navarre will only be interested in serious players, anyway," Afia replied.

She watched the woman nod, slide out of the booth, and vanish into the crowd, taking her one bodyguard with her.

Afia figured she'd come out ahead, and hanging around after this was just wasting time, so she gave the crone a head start, then nodded Bethany into motion.

They swung by the ladies' room on the way out, then emerged into a night dropping down towards cold. Already, she could see her breath steaming in the air as they climbed back up to street level. One of the bouncers had slipped her his comm number as they left, but Afia had no interest in the guy.

Looked like the kind that was self-centered in bed. She'd gotten too spoiled by Javier and a few others to put up with bad sex.

Bethany hung close as they walked, taking a reasonably direct route back to the hotel. Not a lot of foot traffic on the sidewalk, as most people were opting to grab a taxi or at least ride in a vehicle. Meant that they weren't moving with any sort of crowd.

That was fine. Anyone trying to follow her would be in for a surprise. Anybody trying to bother her would really have it coming.

Afia looked up at the sound of a vehicle descending on lifters, right in the middle of the street, and practically sighed with disgust. Folks were predictable in this game.

Junior varsity.

Fuck-wits.

She turned to Bethany and caught the nod of acknowledgment.

"Run," Afia ordered, putting word to deed.

PART 4

Bethany had spent too much time dealing with pissy admirals who thought they remembered something that they'd read in a book, only to later discover that they'd actually seen it in some action/adventure vid. Some character who'd had plot armor and a magical library that could be consulted for the perfect bit of information to instantly solve some puzzle.

Shit like that rarely happened in the real universe, but she'd been far too junior to do anything but stand there with a calm exterior on her face as some idiot with a lot of braid ranted about the failures of a library system he or she had more than likely ordered gutted to save money.

That sort of career left you with a keen understanding of emotional byplay.

She watched Afia turn to the car landing, and saw the woman shift into combat engineer mode, already taking shorter strides as she started speeding up.

"Run," Afia said, and Bethany was already chasing her.

Longer legs barely kept up with the way the short woman

moved. Plus, Bethany took a half moment to draw one of her stunners and carry it in her hand.

Then she was pounding down the sidewalk in Afia's wake, making far more noise than the small woman did. Obviously, she needed classes on moving quietly at some future point. Maybe a change in footwear?

She'd ask Djamila what she should be doing to improve her wardrobe, since firefights on dark sidewalks looked to be a thing Bethany was going to be participating in, going forward.

But then, she'd demanded the right to bloom. Her old professor Dorn Hetzel had accused her of being an unbloomed rose in a letter he'd written to Javier, trying to find her a job.

At least roses had thorns. She might not be blooming yet, but she could still sting.

Afia reached a corner and turned right, Bethany in close pursuit.

Behind them, the vehicle had landed maybe long enough to drop off one person, then taken off again. Probably flying overhead so the driver could make sure they didn't get away.

She wondered what sort of weapon the person chasing them would have. Knife? Beam? Slugthrower?

How badly did they want to capture Afia and Bethany? Or were they out to cut any competition?

Boots slapping on pavement behind her as someone turned a corner. Bethany watched Afia start to weave as she ran, and tried to emulate that. Again, something the Dragoon was going to need to teach her at some point.

Or maybe the taller Dr. St. Kitts should lead the class, since Emma was into martial arts for aerobics as well as combat, teaching classes up to a black belt in a variety of forms.

Djamila took the black belts Emma produced and made them *dangerous*, as she put it.

Might need to be some of that in Bethany's future. She wasn't afraid for her life, but everyone else certainly had a lot more experience at this sort of thing, even if they usually admitted later that they were making it up as they went.

A beam weapon pulse cut the night, sounding like fabric being torn over a public address system. Bethany flinched, expecting something to impact her back, or to suddenly lose control of her limbs and face plant on the damp sidewalk.

Neither happened.

Instead, a man stepped out of an alley, ignoring them completely as he pointed a backpack-mounted DEMP weapon overhead.

Directed ElectroMagnetic Pulse. Stun beams for computers. Miniature versions of the ion pulsars *Excalibur* used on other ships.

Did a number on flying cars, too, as quietly humming lightning suddenly connected the man to it, followed by the car slamming into the ground a moment later like a symphony of anvils being thrown down a flight of stairs.

"We're clear," a voice called from behind them.

Afia slowed and stopped, so Bethany did too.

Turning, Hajna was standing over a figure on the sidewalk, prodding it with a toe while Iqbal kept watch. Two more figures appeared a few moments later. Helmfried and Sascha.

Bethany turned to the man with the portable cannon and caught Demyan's smile.

"Always wanted to do that," he laughed.

Then he shot the car a second time, more lightning playing over the skin as things shorted with a smoldering smoke that suggested internal fires somewhere.

Sascha and Helmfried moved around to the driver's side and tapped the window with blasters. The driver unlocked the door and got dragged out, thrown face-down, and stunned unconscious.

"Flight One," Hajna said aloud. "Lock on these coordinates and descend. Watch the dead aircar in the middle of the street. We don't care if you crush it, but it might be on fire shortly."

"Roger that," Delridge Smith replied.

Already, Bethany could hear a big airtruck starting to drop on their location. Bethany had been told earlier that security was covered, but she'd thought that the Dragoon meant the two pathfinders and their dates.

Obviously, Bethany hadn't been *paranoid enough*.

Something else for the tall woman to teach her.

She watched Del landing and considered how dangerous her new life really was.

Having friends like this, though, did put a smile on her face.

PART 5

Javier studied the two minnows his dangerous net had swept up. Fools had been stunned more than once, then injected with something to keep them calm, quiet, mostly incoherent, and not at all a problem.

There were problems, about the third or fourth time you hit somebody with a stun beam. Medical situations often erupted, requiring medical professionals.

As he was as close to that as anybody here, Javier had better things to do with his time.

But right now, he had a pair of punks in chairs. Hands tied behind them. Ankles tied to the chairs, in case they were feeling frisky. Biosigns read good. Shortly, he'd bring them back to the surface.

First, he needed a moment.

Just pulling the outfit out of the back of the closet and unzipping the storage bag he kept it in brought back a lot of memories. Not all of them were positive ones, but more than he used to have when he'd first put the outfit on.

Captain Eutropio Navarre. *The Killer* himself.

Twenty-ring lace-up boots in glossy neo-leather, with curb-stomping soles and hull-metal toes. Bright red laces all the way up and double-knotted at the top.

Knee-length britches out of dark maroon corduroy, with heavy leather combat padding along the outer edge in case some turd out of a chop-socky movie kicked him. The socks were much lighter fabric today, and only as tall as the boots, rather than covering the knees.

Sixteen-centimeter-tall leather belt around his middle, with a canary-yellow sash tied around that.

Up top, the sleeveless doublet in that same maroon corduroy as the britches, but with two rows of buttons that ran from the inside of his hips to the middle of his collar-bones.

White shirt under the doublet. Long sleeves that covered up all the muscles and hairy bits. He was in way better shape now than he'd been when 'Mina first came up with the costume, so it had been replaced with an improved duplicate.

And just for the hell of it, Javier had kept the cloth tied around his forehead, with a *Neu Berne* Assault Marine logo in the middle. Djamila still flinched when she saw it. The Dragoon had even given Javier one of her old ones to replace the one 'Mina had originally found in a pawn shop somewhere.

It was a look. It had even worked to convince people that he was a sadistic killer.

Killing a lot of people at *Meehu Platform* and *Nidavellir* had helped cement that rep.

But those people had all been pirates. They'd had it coming.

Today, he had to be in character. Earlier than he'd originally planned, but plans like this were best handled like meat. Sometimes a little rare. Hardly ever cooked all the way through.

Small support cast around him today. Hadiiye. Afia and Bethany as his nameless intermediary babe fixers.

And Captain Navarre.

He nodded to Bethany, and the woman cracked open the smelling salts under the nose of the first guy, then the second. Both men. Early twenties. Rough-looking fellows. Tough, at least in their own minds. Minor league players here. Darker than Anglo, but not much. Maybe a shade lighter than Djamila or Bethany. Nothing like him and Afia.

The galaxy was filled with shades of humanity, but people tended to colonize new worlds with like-minded folks, which often had meant culturally and ethnically similar as well.

Captain Navarre was a Hispanic killer, descended from Spanish royalty. The House of Aritza was the ruling house of Navarre from 824 to 1234 CE, so a little over six thousand years ago. And it wasn't like Javier didn't know that history.

The driver came around first. They had names. Javier didn't care. Navarre wouldn't have cared, even before he became a little less xenocidal as a result of meeting the perfect woman.

The punk who had been chasing Afia and Bethany on foot looked like the junior player here, anyway.

Eyes took a while coming into focus. Javier had left the lights on their normal setting. Rude, but again, in character. Really rude would have been shining it directly into their faces.

They hadn't done anything to piss him off.

Yet.

Slowly, those two minds engaged as well. They tried to move and found they couldn't. Considered speaking and counted the number of guns around them.

And the amazing deadly woman behind him.

That had been Wilhelmina Teague, the first time. Djamila had been able to get over most of her body issues and introversion to step up into the role later, when that second mission had involved walking around a resort ship completely nude, or with a cloth tied loosely around her hips and nothing more.

'Mina was about one hundred and ninety centimeters tall normally—a little taller than Javier—to which she had added fourteen-centimeter platforms and heels.

Djamila Sykora was shorter than all her male kin, and still two hundred and ten centimeters tall in her bare feet. She'd tweaked the boots and only walked around with six centimeters of leather and tread underneath. Still enough that Javier looked up at her from about in the center of her sternum.

Tall, though. Impossibly tall. Long legs poured into pointy-toed, high-heeled boots that came up past her knees. In a color of sparkly, bright purple that was almost mesmerizing to look at. More mesmerizing than Djamila normally ever attempted on her own.

Cream-colored tights that showed off the powerful thigh muscles the woman had from running up and down decks with heavy gear packs every day.

A belted tunic, dangling just past her bottom if she were to slowly spin in place. Perhaps showing off. Javier always thought of it as chamois, it had that feel. It was the color of doves in a fog.

Around her waist, Hadiiye wore a fancy sash/girdle/belt/thingee in a black so dark that it seemed to absorb light. Because he had convinced 'Mina originally that pirates always wore fancy sashes. Every movie agreed on that.

Glossy black leather bandoliers attached to a brass ring that rested exactly between her breasts, at the level of her nipples, and focused the eyes on the deep V of her top, straining to hold those breasts in. She had nice breasts, struggling to be free. 'Mina's had been much larger, so they'd gotten squished up. Here, Djamila's pectoral muscles became obvious.

It always took Javier several moments of looking at the

woman—women—to remember Hadiiye had a face. A layer of makeup base to make her look vaguely Egyptian, an effect heightened with the brown eye-liner and color. Blood-red lips that made her look like a night creature. Mixed with the now-dark hair, she was someone else. And most men would never make it that far north, anyway, to actually see her face. He certainly didn't often feel that great of a need, even with Djamila playing the role.

Both men locked onto Hadiiye first, as intended. Part of that outfit was to distract. 'Mina had been pretty damned good in the role of a bodyguard for the infamous Navarre. Djamila Sykora was simply the most dangerous human being Javier had ever met in a lifetime of questionable decisions.

And she knew it.

He heard the way her boots squeaked as she flexed and stepped closer to her latest victims, like a black widow spider. Not a praying mantis, because she wouldn't be interested in bedding junior varsity punks like this.

Hell, it had taken Afia, Suvi, and some blackmail to finally get Djamila to admit how she felt about Zakhar long enough to do something about it. Hadiiye was different, though. She might use that body offensively in a sexual way, if the mission called for it.

Like him, she was occupying a role for a short period of time. Nothing more.

It wasn't who they were.

Still, she sold it well. Walked around behind the two men and rested a possessive hand on each outer shoulder. The two were close enough that she could crack their skulls together if she wanted.

And she was strong enough.

Javier let the two stew for another moment before he drew a breath loud enough to break the tableaux.

"I'm Navarre," he announced. "You're on my shit list. Who are you and why shouldn't I kill you?"

Hard. Rude. Lethal.

But this was also the character who had killed *Salekhard*, even if 'Mina had fired the actual shot that ruptured the biowarfare container into the ship's life support system and Zakhar had killed it with ship's cannons.

Navarre'd still gotten all the credit.

And all the fear.

"Boss just wanted to know who the ladies worked for," the driver said carefully, his voice cracking about halfway and going up a musical third.

"Right now, they work for me," Javier growled, sliding deeper into that killer's mindset. "I hired them to find me some things. Your boss anybody important enough to bother with, or are you two-bit punks nobody will even miss?"

Wasn't like he couldn't toss them in the brig for a while, then drop them on some other planet with money and no identification cards. He'd done that more than once. Djamila's idea, but it worked.

"He's one of the biggest bosses in Valadris City," the driver replied.

The punk next to him was wisely staying silent. Might protect him.

Might not.

"That's nice," Navarre sneered at the men. "Who cares? Still, I'm not here to kill everyone on *Valadris*. In fact, I'm being especially friendly with the locals. At least until they give me a reason to get vicious. There's always that. So instead of dumping your bodies out the airlock to deorbit, I might as well use you to send a message the old fashioned way. One, stay out of my way. You tell your boss that. Two, I'm right here in orbit. If he wants to be polite, I'll talk. If he wants trouble, I've got that covered, too."

"Three," Hadiiye spoke up suddenly. "If I or my people ever see either of you again, we'll assume self-defense and just open fire. With lethal weapons next time. That's the only warning you get, so maybe the two of you should talk to your boss, then book a trip to Earth or someplace equally distant so we don't happen to run into you again. Am I clear?"

Djamila Sykora sounded like a *Neu Berne* Assault Marine when she said shit like that. Because she had been.

Hadiiye added a slow, romantic burn to the tones. Seductive, right up until the content became clear. About where she'd cut your throat, then lick your blood off the blade as she watched you die.

If he didn't know her any better…

Javier kept his scowl intense enough to etch hull-metal. Those two might piss themselves if she pushed any harder, but she also seemed to know exactly where that line was.

So unlike the woman who had shot him the first time they'd met.

The two nodded like their heads might fall off.

Javier had other things he might have said. Other threats to get them to behave.

Nothing he could say right now would look anything but weak after what Hadiiye had just done, so he turned to Afia.

"Drop them on the planet safely," he said simply. "Their boss can be helpful, or he can stay out of my way."

Javier nodded to Djamila and turned towards the hatch.

Exit, stage left, pursued by a bear. Except that he was being followed by a killer even worse than him.

Maybe. She shot people with a grace and skill that still astounded him, but Javier didn't suppose that she would have killed *Salekhard* like he had. Or done things at *Nidavellir* the same way.

Navarre-the-killer was still the biggest threat to the peace of mind of this galaxy.

PART 6

Zakhar sat behind his desk with a glass of whiskey sour on the rocks and watched patiently as Javier growled, stomped, cussed, and generally got it out of his system.

Man was a killer, but only a tiny, inner circle ever got to see the costs Javier paid for going there. For being Captain Navarre.

"I did not come here to start a gang war with the local underworld," Javier griped.

Zakhar toasted the man silently, watching Javier remember that he had his own glass. They both sipped. It seemed to help Javier relax.

The *Bryce Connection*. Two *Concord* naval officers. Brothers under the skin who had been there. Done that. Bore the scars. Saved the galaxy.

"You don't have to," Zakhar reminded him. "Afia sold them a bill of goods about you moving into this sector and trying to be nice to folks."

"They won't fall for it for long," Javier grimaced. "The ego necessary to get to the top of those sorts of organizations means that they have to readjust the entire hierarchy around here to accommodate us."

"Most of them can't take on Suvi," Zakhar noted dryly, taking another sip. "They'll have one or two small warships capable of threatening even armed freighters. Nothing like *Excalibur*. Hell, only *Syntha* is dangerous to us, and then only because they stumbled into a gap we can't cover without a lot of planning, luck, and maybe a refit to add a whole series of pulse weapons good enough to swat hornets."

"We're still likely to have to fight a small war," Javier said.

"Only if you're intent on staying around these sectors," Zakhar said. "I seem to remember your comment to Djamila about being the cowboy from the old pre-industrial era. Ride into town with the opening credits. Shoot the bad guys. Save everyone. Ride out with the closing music. Something about saving the galaxy?"

"There are times I hate you," Javier said dryly. "Especially when you're right. How do we handle this in such a way that Navarre's reputation stays intact? Without anybody whispering that he's gone soft?"

"After what you plan to do to the pirates of *Syntha*?" Zakhar laughed uproariously. "Javier, nobody is going to think you've gone weak. Totally, freaking insane, maybe, but that's another tool in your box when you need it. Maybe you'll have to go rob a bank after this, to remind them of *Shangdu* and the fact that Navarre can also be subtle when he needs to be. We have a lot of options. And Suvi can handle most fools herself. Isn't that right, Yeoman?"

He watched her screen come live on the wall beside the door. Right where she'd be if she was sitting in the other chair. Made her look more like a crew member when she did that.

Which was why he'd had his office adjusted.

"Aye, sir," she replied.

Suvi was *Sentient*. A computer program controlling the entire vessel. And more human than any other ship he'd ever known. That was Javier reprogramming her when it had just been the two of them. Plus that first generation of chickens, who were all gone now, with more replacing them to provide fresh eggs for the kitchen on a daily basis.

"Suvi, I want you to start an analysis of all orbital traffic around *Valadris*," Zakhar said. "Or extend the one you have. Rate every vessel on a threat chart you invent, with a theoretical Class III Warmaster at the top and you in the second tier with a Class II like your old cousin *Meridian*. Keep it updated as new ships arrive, but assume anybody leaving might return."

"Aye, Captain," Suvi grinned. "Would you like every other planet we've visited on that chart as well?"

Zakhar snorted. She was, of course, way ahead of him.

"Keep them as tabs on a spreadsheet," he grinned. She grinned back. He turned to Javier. "Anybody causes me or her grief gets the Navarre-the-killer stomping. Just like *Nidavellir*. Relax on that front and worry about how you're going to take down *Syntha*. I think you're crazy, but I've known that since I met you. Have you bit off too much this time?"

"Maybe," Javier shrugged, which astonished Zakhar. He never admitted failure. "At the same time, I got you two. And Hadiiye. Afia and Bethany. Iqbal and his Bunnies. Del. Shit, it's like we're a combat operation masquerading as a diplomatic mission or something."

"Or something," Zakhar acknowledged. "The Khatum laid down strict rules for me, separate from what she told you."

He watched Javier perk up at that. Behnam had sat in that same chair, orbiting *Altai*, and worried like a wife sending her sailor husband off, rather than a planetary ruler commissioning a ship.

"You are to come back safely to her, she ordered," Zakhar said. "And that I and my people were to move heaven and earth to accomplish that. I already had most of the folks I needed. She gave me the budget and connections to add a few more. It's your ship, but it's my command, Javier. You decided that we needed to save the folks of *Byormi* from pirates. So we're going to."

"Simple as that?" Javier asked.

Zakhar laughed.

"It's you, Javier," he replied. "Is it ever as simple as that?"

The man shrugged. Grinned. Finished his drink. Zakhar did the same.

It was never as simple as that.

But they'd do their damnedest. And that had been pretty damned good so far.

PART 7

Bethany was forward in her library. Hers, because Javier had offered her a cubic volume into which to put actual books and other trophies as part of this voyage. Mostly, a handful of study carrels, book scanners, and comfortable chairs and couches where someone could sit with their reader and a mug of coffee or something while reading one of the million or so electronic books Suvi had accumulated, with budgets for more at every stop.

Something about Javier's theory that you learned about a culture by watching popular movies and reading bestselling books. The stories they told about themselves, both as heroes as well as villains.

Valadris had a sophisticated planetary communications network. Not quite *Concord* standards, but better than most around here. Supposedly the most advanced in the region, though, with others sliding off the scale into backwards farm country in a hurry.

But it was her library. Javier and Zakhar had made it clear that she owned this space of the ship, and gave her a purchasing budget to keep it updated. Most of that money went into book dumps for Suvi, naturally. And for the crew to consume at a much more leisurely pace.

Bethany was stretched out comfortably under a blanket, turned sideways on her favorite couch. In addition, she usually kept the air in here a degree or three cooler than everywhere else, just because hot cocoa and a blanket was so soothing. Especially today.

Javier entered to jar her out of her comfort.

Well, not Javier. Technically, Captain Navarre. The killer who she had first heard about, then later met. Then gotten hired by.

Who turned out to be a renegade botanist. And a pretty good boss.

The Navarre outfit, as Afia had warned her, made him look hot. Even as old as the man was, sixteen years her senior. Most admirals that age were fat and out of shape. Javier could probably walk her into the ground, and she was in better shape now than she'd been on active duty.

She studied him as he approached, with a single raised eyebrow and a finger already marking her page with her bookmark resting on the back of the couch.

Navarre moved to the chair and sat without speaking. Javier was already generally quiet around her. Navarre took it up a whole extra level.

Bethany grabbed the bookmark and set her book on the floor, trading it for the travel mug of hot cocoa. Probably should have added a hit of rum, from the look on his face, but she just smiled innocently at him.

A librarian, dealing with an unruly and possibly unhappy admiral.

Not the first time.

"Tell me about *Valadris*," he said after a moment of stretched, pregnant silence. "Who do they want to be when they grow up?"

Bethany marshaled her thoughts. Not the first time they'd done this, but the first for this world.

"Oldest sibling of a brood," she replied slowly, feeling through the two books she'd finished since hitting orbit, then being able to visit used bookstores on the surface. "This region are all the cousins and family of a clan that never moves far when they get out of school and turn into adults. Culturally, almost incestuous, but that's mostly being off the sorts of major trade routes where Cornell and Nita went looking. Should you be asking them?"

The two strangers were aboard. Traveling almost in style, but largely staying out of the way. They would remain behind on *Valadris*, arranging their own passage back to *Byormi*, with an expectation that *Excalibur* would hopefully visit when the mission was complete.

Farmers, more than anything. Not a married couple. Not even dating. Bethany thought that Cornell maybe didn't like girls at all and Nita hadn't pushed him.

The woman had a crew of pirates if she needed to scratch an itch. Bethany did as well. Just didn't explore it very often. Officer, around too many enlisted people. And the one that might be the most interesting was her boss. Sitting across from her. Carbonating her hormones, if she had to give it a term.

"They don't know this region of space," Navarre replied. "*Byormi* is only loosely connected, and then because they send more trade goods to *Valadris* than to any of the bigger worlds. Mostly, that's food and primary goods for money. Who is *Valadris*?"

"Port city to the hinterlands that the other planets represent," Bethany replied.

His eyes lit up at that, so she figured she'd found the right description. You sent goods down the river or over the road network to *Valadris*. They had the factories to turn all that into finished goods they sold back to you on your farm.

"And *Syntha* is the unruly cousin who just got out after doing three years for assault and bank robbery," Navarre nodded. "On parole, but the parole officer is a drunk who rarely reads the news. Plus, the cops are too busy over here to want to go knock on your door and maybe get shot trying to execute an arrest warrant."

"As good an analogy as any," she agreed. "Crime here is lower per capita than elsewhere, but *Valadris* has up to one hundred or more times the population, and all the issues of the big city. I suspect that *Syntha* is working a deal with locals here to act as their fence but I can't find the evidence I'd need to point fingers. Definitely buying stolen goods, though, because Suvi has been tracking cargo against gross planetary product and it doesn't match up. Plus, I cannot think of anything more demoralizing to a pirate than having to haul away a million tons of wheat, then grinding it, then processing it, then baking it. Locals here are buying things cheaper than market."

"Too much like work," Navarre laughed. "They just want the croissant, not the effort of making it from the planting upward. To say nothing of raising the cattle to provide the milk to make the butter."

"Does it matter?" Bethany asked, watching the man for clues.

"I'm not sure yet," Navarre replied. "Fixing *Syntha* to save *Byormi* might require fixing *Valadris* as well. Otherwise somebody else steps in after we leave and takes the ecological niche those pirates are currently holding."

Bethany stirred, trying to find the right words.

"Talk," Navarre-the-killer ordered in that hard, deadly voice he did when he forgot who he was.

"In other places..." she trailed off, shaking her head for a moment. "In other systems, that level of corruption absolutely requires official sanction, however much under the table. Too many things going on to keep it quiet. As you said, the parole officer would have to be a drunk to miss it. Not necessarily pirates in a league with Walvisbaai, or H & W Heavy Industries, or even your old bosses in the Jarre Foundation, but there will be elected officials on the take. And bureaucrats working the margins to protect things in return for a cut or a stack of kickbacks."

"You're thinking we can't fix it?" Navarre asked.

"Maybe not without spilling blood," Bethany replied. "I suspect that to be on your docket for *Syntha*, but were you thinking you needed to clean up *Valadris* before we left the region?"

"Zakhar asked if I was here to shoot all the bad guys," Navarre mused.

"Might be the only way you could actually do it," Bethany said. "Is it worth it?"

"There are always three answers to that question, Bethany," the man said, sitting straighter and suddenly less Navarre-the-killer. Probably more like the goofball botanist might have been, if early in his career a few things had gone a different direction. "First, if I rescue a stray kitten, I haven't dealt with the breakdown in social systems that cause stray cats to be running around your city. And probably wild dogs or raccoons or coyotes that will feed on little cats. Second, I haven't gotten the mama cat fixed, such that she stops having litters regularly, so the ecosystem continues unabated and entropy suggests a gradual worsening over time. But third, and this is always the key point, I have absolutely changed the life of that one cat from being scared and alone and facing predators, to living in a warm house with regular food and love. For that cat, I have changed the world. I can't fix *Syntha*. I probably can't do anything important about *Valadris*. Not without putting in more effort and maybe doing more damage than I do good."

"So we're back to *Kimmeria*?" Bethany asked.

They'd identified the derelict ship. Found it. Studied it to determine that it was no threat to the modern age. Then handed it off to folks who would hopefully turn it into a museum and breeding zoo for the cute, little tree 'roos that were in the process of evolving into a new species.

"Maybe," Navarre said. Except that Javier was speaking now, not the killer. "If we can show people a better way to do things. And kill the ones who refuse to live as civilized folk. That might include locals on *Valadris*, after we're done on *Syntha*, so I want you going deep enough to be able to estimate what any given death does. Not the person, but the rank. If I end up killing a governor who's utterly corrupt, that's a lot bigger than a quiet assassination of a career bureaucrat in an office so small and remote that they hardly show up on an org chart, except down in a forgotten corner."

"Should you look at maybe kidnapping a journalist?" Bethany asked.

"Talk to me." *Navarre* was back.

"I think that, for this planet, publicity might be just as good a weapon as a blaster," Bethany said. "At least as far as your needs in this situation. What if we found a muckraker to go with us to *Syntha* and document all that, then come back here and dig into the folks who have to be acting as fences and protectors for the pirates on *Valadris*? Put it on the front page with pictures, databases, and maybe confessions?"

"Find me that person," Navarre said.

He rose abruptly and walked to the door, pausing to look back at her and nod once.

She'd probably just saved any number of lives. Folks who would never know it.

After all, if you studied history at all, you quickly understood that violence, while it might solve *every* problem, was *rarely* the best possible solution.

Sometimes sunlight worked better.

Then she was alone in her library.

"Suvi," she said, causing the woman to invest herself

more fully in one of the shards she had constantly monitoring every room on the ship. The cute blond appeared on a nearby screen, smiling at her.

"I like it," she said simply, telling Bethany that between one heartbeat and the next she had reviewed the conversation with Navarre. Digested it. Approved of it.

"Find me a list of local reporters who might fit the characteristics we need," Bethany said. "Sharp. Smart. Young. Hostile to the existing power structure of *Valadris* to the point they'd be willing to rock the boat. Progressives who think they can save the galaxy yet, who haven't gotten old enough to rethink it. Get me the names, then you and I will start sorting them and culling until we have a few we can approach."

"Gonna light *Valadris* on fire?" Suvi asked hopefully.

"Gonna try," Bethany promised.

VALADRIS PORT

PART 1

Stacia looked at the message again and wondered if it was for real. If she'd learned anything in her twenty-four years, *too good to be true* usually was. Still, whoever had crafted that message had an amazingly precise understanding of human nature.

Or at least hers. The hook was metaphorically set and Stacia didn't think that there was anything anybody could do about it.

A time and a place. Middle of the afternoon. A restaurant not far from her office. Offer of a documentarian job, with whoever was behind it offering her a stipend just to show up and talk to them. And about what she made in a week in her daily job. Granted, the *Valadris Beacon* could hardly afford to pay her much. At the same time, she had her own money that let her work for them cheap.

For a cause.

But someone had transferred funds into her account, unasked, along with an invitation to meet them for lunch, in public, at a place with a lot of windows and good foot traffic.

Stacia knew she'd pissed off a few of the more powerful players on this planet, but didn't think that any of them had risen to the level of sending goons to kill her or even beat her up.

Still, she had her friend Jessilyria sitting across the restaurant, comm handy and ready to call for help or even just scream bloody murder if necessary.

Always have a friend watching your back.

Stacia looked around from her booth, checked the time on her comm, then ran a hand back through her blonde, pageboy cut. She'd dressed nicer than normal. And knew she was cute, but not traffic-stopping. Too short. Too skinny. Too smart for most of the men to be interested in, once they got to know her.

That big mouth opened and bigger words came out. And they weren't all about sportsball or beer.

She had bigger dreams.

The glass door to the restaurant opened and a man entered. They locked eyes across the distance, then he started her way.

At first glance, she would have said her dad's age, but he was in fantastic shape. Trim and muscular. Dark in a Hispanic way, just starting to gray along the edges. Clean shaven. Hard face. Flat stomach.

There was a woman with him. Much younger. Maybe late twenties. Light brown hair darker than Stacia's and darker than Jessilyria's. Tall. Hot.

They approached the table, the man in the lead and looming over her in a polite way.

"McNulty?" he asked so quietly that folks in the next booth might have missed it, if someone was sitting there.

"That's right," Stacia nodded.

The man turned to the woman. The tall woman slid into the booth across from Stacia, then the man followed.

"This is Bethany," he said, introducing the tall woman and not himself, which Stacia found telling. "She tells me that you might be the perfect person to meet my needs. I'm going to go somewhere, and do something. Then probably come back here later and do more things. From the outside, some of those things are going to upset some people. Maybe anger them. I don't really care. They deserve it already, and I have only just begun researching my target."

He paused there, both of them studying Stacia's face. She studied them.

The woman had the look of an academic. A scholar. Stacia had just finished a double-major in journalism and political science, and was contemplating advanced degree work next. She knew professors and such. This woman wasn't, but had spent a lot of time around them.

The man...

"You haven't introduced yourself," Stacia challenged the man. Politely. Enough to see if they could find margins.

"I have not," he agreed. "My name would cause you to wander down the wrong rabbit hole at this moment. Would spoil your usefulness for my needs. The job requires a documentarian. A person skilled at taking footage, records, evidence, and whatever else we find, and turning it into a court case. Except that this will be the court of public opinion, because none of the players likely to be swept up in my net will be criminally prosecuted. At least not until much, *much* later, and then only assuming that you did your job successfully."

Again, that pause.

Dump a chunk of information, then let her absorb it before continuing. The man had an excellent way with people. Stacia found herself leaning in.

"You want someone destroyed socially?" she asked, glancing back and forth at the two.

The woman nodded, but was very obviously not in charge. He was.

"I don't know who they are yet," he admitted. "Or where to find them. But I know they exist. I know they are engaged in some level of criminal conspiracy off-world. I know that, in going to that other place to deal with problem children over there, I'm likely to find clues and evidence that leads me back here. I'd like to take down the ringleaders on both ends of that equation. However, I'm not a local. And don't really intend to remain around afterwards, because my presence will obfuscate things and cause people to react poorly."

Stacia parsed his words. All of them. Lots of data. Almost no information. Hell of a framework, though. Got her journalism nose sniffing trail and she didn't even have a scent yet.

"Why do you want me?" she asked sharply, just to see what else he might let her know.

"Bethany tells me that you hit all my requirements," the man said. "Young, progressive, smart, educated. Connected socially to bigger players because a newspaper like the *Valadris Beacon* is too small for you to remain at long. Unless you decide to make it a career. I asked her to find me a fearless muckraker on *Valadris*. She chopped the list down from one hundred names to five. You are the first person I wanted to talk to, but I have four others. None of them are as good as you, from what I've read of your work over the last year."

Stacia *considered*. The implications were at once fairly clear, and also pretty damning.

"You are going to go after some criminal conspiracy?" she confirmed his words.

The man nodded.

"And you want their crimes documented?" she pressed.

"I want their destruction recorded and documented," he corrected her, voice dropping down a shade and sounding more like a rusty knife. "I want their friends on *Valadris* prosecuted, either by you and all your friends, or by the government. I won't know what your likely outcomes are until I finish the first half of my job. You are the reporter with the ultimate pool assignment, if I understand the terminology, because your name will be first on the list of folks when your video and stories come out. Your byline. Your fame. I fully intend to vanish after my parts are done, so you'll have to fight your own wars. That was also one of the requirements I put to Bethany. Someone who could take on all of *Valadris*. And would."

"Who are you going after?" Stacia asked, utterly intrigued now, in spite of her instincts to dig into the man's own secrets.

"Can I ask you to remain silent, even if we can't come to an employment agreement?" he asked.

"Technically, you'd paid me as much as I make in a week at the Beacon, just to meet you for lunch," she said.

And then the waiter approached and distracted everything. Stacia started lists in her head so she didn't forget anything, as everyone got coffee and menus.

She knew the place, so she didn't need to read more than to glance.

"What's good?" Bethany asked.

"I was getting a chicken tika masala," Stacia replied automatically, wondering what these folks might want.

The food was a wide mix of things often referred to simply as Galactic, since it had fused several ways on Earth before leaving, then mixed several more times as it spread via the many waves of colonization over the millennia.

"Staying with a burger," the man said. "Greasy and all the fixings."

"Gosh?" Bethany asked. "You? So out of character."

Stacia so wanted to ask who that character was. Was it a character? The man was layers of intriguing, but way too old for her to be interested in.

Bethany, however…

In the end, Bethany tried the tika as well. The waiter got their orders, then understood to leave them alone until the food was ready. He nodded and withdrew to the far end of the place. Not a lot of customers, but it was mid-afternoon.

She studied the man again. Still.

"Silence, if this doesn't work out and you walk away?" he asked again.

"Okay," Stacia agreed. Tentatively. Maybe she'd mentally crossed her fingers in the process.

It depends.

How many times had she heard that phrase?

"My goal is to go to *Syntha* and end the pirates as a problem," he said simply. Quietly. Privately.

Stacia gasped. Goggled. Mouth catching flies and everything.

Shit.

He nodded. Bethany even grinned, like she'd been expecting this reaction.

Stacia took a moment and got everything organized again.

Then the implications hit her like a ton of bricks.

He'd said he was going somewhere else, and dealing with a problem. Then expecting her to come back here with evidence that folks on *Valadris* were involved. Evidence Stacia would use to destroy someone's reputation locally, because this man thought that they might be otherwise untouchable.

If it was the *Syntha* pirates, he might be right.

The audacity of it all took her breath away. And excited her. She might be in a position to actually do something about all the corruption everyone tacitly acknowledged, but didn't do anything about.

Might clean up *Valadris*. Or burn it to the ground. You kinda needed to do the latter to manage the former, most of the time.

She studied the man closer. Again noted the age somewhere in his early forties. The calmness. The deadly serious intent in his eyes.

He wasn't going to *Syntha* and hoping he could do something. In his mind, he'd already destroyed those pirates as a problem and just hadn't told her or anybody else how he had done it yet.

Wow.

"Okay, I have ten thousand questions," she finally managed, mind racing as fast as it would go.

He started to speak and she waved him off.

"Yes, I realize you don't know most of the answers," she acknowledged. "Not yet. But you think it can be done. You want it documented. You want that evidence coming back here to be used as a weapon. You want me holding that weapon, because you don't want to be known for it."

He nodded. Bethany grinned, like she'd already gamed this out and convinced her stubborn boss to do this. Like he might not believe either of them.

"Who are you?" she whispered.

Bethany's face lit up. The man scowled. Stacia wondered if a bet was going to be paid off after this.

He leaned forward, face as intense as it was deadly.

"I'm going to say a name," he said. "Between you and me and Bethany, it will be a powerful name. However, you need to be aware that it is not who I am. It is a character that was invented several years ago, because I needed to do some things to some people at that time, and needed it not traced back to me. It also needs to remain private for now. Later, you can do with it what you want. After I'm gone. Are we clear?"

Stacia gulped, wondering if they were about to draw knives and seal a blood oath as part of an initiation or something. This had gone far beyond anything Stacia had imagined, even at her weirdest moment, when reading that initial message.

Stacia nodded, unwilling to trust her voice.

"The person going after the pirates is a much worse pirate," he said. "Much deadlier. But this thing needs to be done, and nobody else has the time, energy, and willingness to do it. I've been accused, by Bethany and others you will meet if you take this job, of being a cowboy. Of riding in like they do in those ancient vids, shooting the bad guys, then riding off into the sunset. That is not without truth, but the story is so much more than that. I'm not doing this by myself. I have an entire team of people helping, and could not do it without all of them. If you take this job, you will be part of that team. You will be expected to act like it. The pay will be far better than the Beacon is giving you, and you might take a leave of absence, just so they can hire a stringer while you are away. I know what their finances are like. You'll document everything. Interview players. Record it all. Bring it back here. Destroy lives that need to be destroyed."

"Who are you, that you think me knowing your name will cause me to run screaming from this restaurant?" Stacia demanded in a hard, nervous whisper.

He was getting to her with all the secrecy and heavy-handedness. Not that she would ever admit it.

He smiled. It was a charming smile, as long as you weren't looking at his eyes.

"Navarre," he replied.

Stacia felt like someone had just punched her in the stomach. Even here, she'd heard stories bubbling out from the *Concord*. The deaths. The savagery. The legend.

Then, she couldn't help it. The journalist kicked in.

Navarre wasn't real? Some kind of cover? Who was the man behind it? Why was he doing these things?

And Stacia knew that there was only one way she would ever find those answers. Ever satisfy that journalistic itch.

"Okay," she said. "I'm in."

Inwardly, she quailed at the lunacy of it all.

What the hell was she getting herself into?

PART 2

Javier sat on his hotel bed with his shoes off and his fingers laced behind his head. Djamila paced. Afia was on the other bed. Bethany sat in the corner at the desk.

That burger had been pretty good. Not great. Satisfying.

"Was the friend ever a threat?" he asked the tall Amazon.

"She was there to cover McNulty in a dangerous situation," Djamila replied. "At least as they might have understood it. She watched intently, but beyond calling the police, I'm not sure what usefulness she might have brought to the situation."

"Not everyone understands warfare, Dragoon," he laughed. "Certainly not like you and yours conduct it. Stacia and her friend were treating it like a blind date, which it was in many ways. Keep a wingmate close who can call for help. Who knows where you are and who you are with. I assume they got pictures of me. Bethany, make sure those get deleted. Navarre can be interviewed, but we'll want his face hidden and his voice masked. The rest of you will make your own decisions on immortality."

"Already working with Suvi on that," Bethany nodded. "She's watched too many true crime shows. Apparently, it's a thing on *Valadris*, which was why we could do this here easier than on some other worlds."

Javier nodded. He didn't have to be perfect. Or even smart. Just lucky. Looking at the three women supporting his insanity, he was certainly the luckiest mug around.

"So she's in," Afia said. "We get her aboard *Excalibur* as soon as she's packed, then head out?"

"Did those other two punks we picked up give you any trouble?" Javier asked.

Djamila laughed. Afia scowled at the tall woman.

"They were properly chastened," Afia said in a sideways sort of voice. "I don't think they'll stop running after they update their boss. It's the old woman who I'm waiting for."

"I thought she sent you some information," Bethany spoke up.

"Not enough," Afia said. "Not for the trade of what she got. Rubs me the wrong way to let her off cheap."

"Do we introduce her to Stacia?" Javier asked.

He really enjoyed the way all three heads snapped around to boggle at him. Gotta keep these three on their toes, ya know.

"Isn't that exactly the wrong thing?" Djamila asked. "Muckraker journalist and criminal organization? I was under the impression that those sorts of groups were generally enemies?"

Afia's eyes got cagey. Which was just one of the things he loved about her.

"You certain she's going to need friends?" Afia asked him.

"Navarre commands a certain respect," Javier volleyed back at her. "And then that crazy son of a bitch is going to go blow up more pirates. Zakhar thinks I might need to plan and execute a bank robbery at some point later, just so folks don't think I've turned into a hero after this."

"Robin Hood robbed the rich," Bethany grinned at him.

"Then you'll need to find me another *Shangdu*," he laughed. "Preferably without its own Behnam. I'm already surrounded by amazing women. Don't really think it would be fair to find more."

Bethany rolled her eyes at him. The others did as well.

Life was good. Completely insane and nowhere near what he'd been expecting at any point longer than two years ago, but fantastic.

"So yeah, I agree with Javier," Afia said after a beat. "If Stacia's in, she needs to meet the old woman. Get connected with her organization in a formal way. Especially if she'll be without cover after we go."

"Her parents have money," Bethany pointed out. "And connections."

"Won't be enough if we end up having to destroy the Governor or folks at that kind of power level," Javier replied. "For them, it's like oxygen. Like the greatest high they ever got from sex, drugs, or music. If we threaten that, they might get ugly. Stacia will need protection and I doubt she really understands that yet. Not seasoned enough yet."

"I'll make a few calls," Afia said. "Can I drag you into a meeting in your badass gear? Both you and Hadiiye? That will make the impression I think Navarre needs, in order to leave his steel-toed bootprint on *Valadris*."

Javier considered it. Afia was one of the sneakiest people he knew. And sharpest. There was a reason she usually handled planetside resupply for Zakhar. Not everything on your wish list was always available from the warehouse.

Sometimes, you had to get *creative*. It helped if you knew a guy who had a cousin. Or how to find him.

"Yeah," he replied. "You set up a meeting. We'll come in hard and heavy. Let the old woman become my primary contact on *Valadris*, mostly because she didn't send punks after you two. Stacia can inherit some of that when we're gone. Hopefully, it will help."

"What if she wants to join the crew after we're done here?" Bethany asked.

It was Javier's turn to turn and gawk.

Bethany grinned. Paybacks could be a bitch.

"No," Javier said simply. "She has a job. I presume that we won't find enough to simply allow some cop to arrest everyone and put them away, so she's got to come back here and put all that to work. Stuff like that takes time. Justice always grinds slower than you expect it to, right until the last minute."

"And later?" Bethany asked.

Javier didn't know where the woman was going. Neither did Djamila or Afia from the looks on their faces.

"If she wants to haul her ass out to *Altai* after us, that's up to her," he decided. "We're nearly a quarter of the way around the galactic disk at that point, so she'll have to make that decision on her own, then put a year into commercial flights to get there. We can fly faster because we're not generally stopping longer than resupply at most worlds. It's only the interesting places, like *Ninovskaya* or *Valadris*, that cause us to really pause on our way home."

Bethany nodded. Javier had once thought that his charm and awesomeness would draw in all the chicks, but he'd long since gotten over himself. Passing forty meant that he was generally invisible to the younger ones, anyway; Afia and a few like her notwithstanding. Mostly, they needed to learn to appreciate competence over looks.

Then he was back in the competition. Or something. Nobody was going to come close to Behnam, but she was also smart enough to understand that she had his heart and his soul. The others could have his body.

Not that he'd ever touched Bethany. Or Djamila.

The women studied him for a long moment, then came to a consensus.

Afia slid off the other bed and put her shoes on.

"I need to make some calls," she announced, turning to scowl at him and Djamila. "You two will rely on room service or dress as low profile as possible when leaving these rooms."

Javier nodded. This was Afia's gig until Navarre-the-killer needed to make an appearance.

Bethany rose as well, following Afia out.

He was alone with Djamila.

Once his worst enemy in the galaxy. Now, one of his closest friends.

Weird.

"I'd ask if you knew what you were doing," she said with a wry grin. "But I already know the answer to that. Will it matter in the long run?"

"Define long," Javier replied. "In however many billion years, the stars will all burn out, leaving nothing but endless darkness. In a few thousand years, all of the civilizations you can think of around us will have collapsed and been reborn into something else. In another couple of centuries, none of us but Suvi will be alive, and nobody has yet proven the Afterlife is anything but a fantasy."

"And today?" she asked, sobering.

"Today, there are bad people doing terrible things to innocents," Javier said. "Zakhar and I were *Concord* Navy. The good guys, at least as we saw it. *Neu Berne* were the bogeymen, but that's just PR. I'm sure you have heroic myths and legends, like King Arthur reborn. That's why *Hammerfield* is called *Excalibur* these days. Save the day and all that. Robin Hood is still spoken of, six thousand years and however many light-centuries removed from his birth. An ancient scholar once stated that all that was necessary for evil to triumph was for good people to do nothing. So no, I can't save *Valadris*. Probably can't save *Syntha*. Might buy *Byormi* time. Maybe other farming worlds. Maybe enough people rise up against the tyranny of might because we set an example. Because we *can* knock off the worst, and maybe the ones left behind aren't able to take control again. Won't know until we try. Won't know in my lifetime if I'm successful."

"The Rising Storm," she nodded.

Javier nodded back.

Dorn was certain it was coming. He had charts, graphs, extrapolations, the works. What he didn't know was *when* it would ignite. *Where. How.*

Why was covered.

"The pressures are building, Djamila," he offered. "We could have all just retired to *Altai* and spent our time around a pool, sipping rum drinks and working on our tans, because *Altai* has a navy big enough to keep brigands and pirates at bay. Not the *Concord* if they got feisty, but that distance is enough for now. The *Concord* is probably fine. *Neu Berne* is fucked, but that's because everyone else is afraid of letting you have a fleet again, after the last time. The *Union of Man* and *Balustrade* are fading powers. Whether some demagogue comes along and promises them a return to imperial glory or something is Dorn's main ignition scenario. It might end up being one of the worlds closer to Earth. They are also old and tired, and maybe looking on the zones that aren't *Union*, *Balustrade*, or *Neu Berne* anymore and wondering if they can carve out their own empire."

"Always empire?" she asked, standing now at the foot of the bed in all her terrible splendor.

The most dangerous person he'd ever met. And that included some interesting folks.

"Human nature," he shrugged. "Folks want power. They accumulate it. It is, however, never enough. So they need more. Addictive. Then they have to pass it on to their kids, because of so many cultural traditions. The kids are never up to the task, so somebody else comes along and takes it away from them. That leads to wars between princes and fools. Innocent people get hurt."

"And saving *Valadris?*" she pressed.

"*Valadris* is the strongest planetary system in the region," Javier said. "Bethany thinks it is the linchpin to the sector and beyond. If we can force them to clean up their act, maybe we buy an entire generation of this area acting like a firebreak against whatever conflagration is coming. Folks who trade with one another are less likely to make war. The rich people who end up controlling too many governments are always afraid that they will lose their fortunes if factories and cities start getting bombed."

"You are a cynical man, Javier," Djamila noted, pausing. "I wish I could say you were wrong."

"Lady, so do I."

PART 3

Afia had set her scowl in place like makeup before going dancing tonight. Hard. Tough. Mean.

The kind of woman who'd had killers coming after her, only to discover that her organization was far more dangerous than anybody had imagined.

Word would get around. Had gotten around. Players in this club were already more respectful. Distant. That would have been a problem if she'd been looking to get lucky, but she had a whole ship of fools up in orbit if she needed that.

Tonight, she was, as she'd quoted earlier, setting *Valadris* up to have Javier's steel-toed, lace-up waffle-stompers leave a permanent and possibly painful imprint on this culture.

As only Navarre might manage.

The old crone had a name. Afia even knew it. But hadn't at the time, so had put out the word that she wanted to see *The Crone* again, and cousins had known who she was after. Probably had ended up awarding the woman a new nickname like a trophy.

Good. *Valadris* wasn't as chauvinistic as some worlds, but

seriously, men screwed things up when you let them pretend to be in charge. At least Javier was smart enough to shut up and let the women in his life run things, without having to pee all over afterward to leave his scent.

Afia growled at the crowded bar in general and waited. As before, she was at the bottom of the round booth, with Bethany on her right. Seriously deadly firepower was stationed a few tables away, with both pathfinders and five of the six Gunbunnies in sight. Only Tom Gruffydd wasn't here, but he was the best driver of the team, so was outside with a low-altitude truck. Del had parked his dangerous self in his primary shuttle at the starport.

Nobody knew if Del had added guns to the thing. Nobody asked the man, either. He had his own superstitions.

For Afia, it was enough to understand that even Suvi might get into the mix if it got bad enough, though that ship should never drop down into an atmosphere. Most couldn't climb out again, but Afia figured the chick had that calculated already.

They'd all been around Javier and Djamila long enough.

Afia sipped. Sealed bottle. Extra expensive. Rowdy club. Loud music. Perfectly safe.

The Crone appeared, emerging from the bodies as if from a fog. No bodyguard with her tonight. None obvious, anyway. Probably assumed she was safe inside Afia's bubble of protection.

Utterly right.

They made a little small talk. Nothing much. Greasing the wheels of comradeship. Afia was set to up this woman's place in the underworld by rubbing off some of Navarre's magic on her.

Needed to make sure that the Crone was prepared for that.

"How can I help tonight?" the Crone asked after a round of generalities.

"Two things," Afia replied.

You didn't have to yell over the music, but you did have to pay attention and frequently read lips as much as hear words.

"Go on."

"Navarre wants to meet you," Afia announced, watching the woman recoil a shade, like someone had touched the back of her neck.

The cold fingers of Death, maybe.

The Crone nodded after a beat hardly long enough to notice. Long enough for someone watching closely, though.

"Second, we've recruited a local journalist to help our mission," Afia continued.

This time, the eyes started confused, then wandered over to concerned.

"Okay."

"She's going with Navarre when he goes to visit *Syntha*," Afia explained, watching the woman's eyes for betrayals. Double-crosses. Stupidity that ended up getting her killed right here in the club before she could spill Javier's plans in the wrong ears.

It was a hard world. Life was cheap and honor expensive.

Afia had also spent more than a decade as a pirate at this point. Not all lovable and friendly like those silly vids liked to make it out, either.

The Crone nodded, head tilted forward so her brows and dark hair seemed to shadow her eyes.

"Then the young woman is coming back here," Afia continued.

"To what purpose?" the Crone asked.

"To destroy whoever is working with those pirates," Afia said, primed for violence if she needed to either punch the woman for drawing a weapon or signal to the pathfinders to take her out.

You got one chance at this, babe.

The Crone processed that information. Took a couple of seconds.

"Navarre doesn't intend to share this sector with them," the Crone said.

Wrong conclusion. Well, technically correct, which was the best kind, but the wrong path to get there.

"Correct," Afia nodded. "It's not big enough for both, so they have to go. He's planning on letting this journalist do a full-on documentary of things, so that she's got the evidence she needs to destroy whoever is fencing for those pirates. If it's your organization involved, or anyone remotely close, I suggest you get up and walk away right now. I'll let you make it to the door alive, but you'll become his nemesis in the morning. Do we understand each other?"

The Crone had been in this business for a long time. She didn't scare easy. She laughed instead.

"I'll enjoy watching those fuckers squirm," she said. "Not sure she can actually take them down, but it will be entertaining."

"Better be," Afia growled. "You'll be helping her."

Boom. Eyes big. Blinking too rapidly. Mental overload.

Better than a punch in the nose to make the brain reboot.

"What?" she managed.

"After Navarre finishes the pirates, he wants your help," Afia said. "He specifically wants to introduce you to the journalist, with an understanding that you'll make yourself and your organization available to help her take down whoever it is that needs to be destroyed for helping those fucks at *Syntha*."

"That's the Governor's office," the woman said, just a trace of fear in her voice.

"Then we'll need a new Governor, won't we?" Afia replied. "One not connected to pirates."

"Why is he doing this?" the Crone demanded in a hurt tone. Lost.

A child who has had a nightmare and wants reassurance that there aren't monsters in the closet, or under the bed.

When there really were.

"He wants this place cleaned up for what he has in mind later," Afia said.

Again, technically true. She couldn't help it if the Crone came to the wrong conclusion about what those ends were.

"Later?" the woman asked anyway.

Afia nodded serenely.

What the hell would a pirate like Navarre need with law and order winning on a planet like this? That was certain to cause any number of people a lot of sleepless nights.

And hey, some of them might decide that now was the time to quietly start moving away from life in a criminal underworld whose days were numbered. Go straight, and all that. Help Stacia clean up this one-horse town.

No, two-horse. *Syntha*, from all the information the old woman had given her, was a one-horse town. *Byormi* didn't even rate that high.

"I'll need to meet Navarre in the flesh," the Crone said after she got her wits locked down and organized again. "Understand his intentions so I can pass it along correctly to my organization."

"Understood," Afia said. "Not here, though. His presence in this system is still generally unknown, and he'd like to keep it that way a bit longer. We need someplace isolated, where he can drop in via shuttle from orbit, have a chat with you specifically, then depart again. He doesn't want to meet your bosses. Or your minions. You, because anyone else is a stranger to him and to me. Are these terms acceptable?"

The woman took a long second to consider. They were asking for the proverbial farmhouse in the middle of nowhere that factored into the early scenes of so many of those horror vids in Suvi's library up on the ship.

You. Alone. Bad monster comes for you. Nowhere to run.

Got the guts to face off with Navarre-the-killer?

"Okay," the Crone said.

91

Her eyes looked another decade older, but her smile had shaved at least that much off her face as she calculated how to twist all this to her personal advantage.

Considering what Afia expected Navarre to do to the woman's mind, that would be good.

Maybe they'd clean this system up before Stacia had to do anything at all.

Afia doubted it.

PART 4

Navarre. It was lacing the boots that put Javier into that dark, deadly state of mind. Not even the headband carried the emotional weight of those boots.

Forecast had called for heavy, chewy rain only a few degrees above freezing, so Adrian had dug out a matching maroon hooded cloak he'd had hidden somewhere. Probably planning for years for this particular look.

Del was flying the shuttle. Because Del. Was even flying like a normal person today, instead of running an assault drop like he frequently did.

There was no reason to come in at those folks on the ground above the speed of sound, then flare back, stall, and slam down onto the landing gear hard enough to dent things.

Though Javier had no doubts whatsoever that Del Smith was the best at that, too.

Across from him, Hadiiye wore a black cloak. Looked like a sail, but only because it had to fit that much woman. Her smile was at once provocative, seductive, and lethal.

Djamila was still in there somewhere, but she'd turned into that other person. He wondered which article of clothing did it for her.

Looking around, Afia was scowling. Bethany phlegmatic. Zakhar intense. All eight of Djamila's killers were in Ops Mode.

Javier had gone ahead and dragged Ilan out of Engineering to accompany him today. Mostly because the Gunbunnies would be outside and otherwise it would be Navarre and Sokolov surrounded by what a fool might mistake for a harem when this meeting went down.

Stacia, sitting directly across from him between Afia and Bethany, certainly seemed to be having second thoughts. Although by now she was probably up to tenth thoughts.

He didn't smile reassuringly, either. Let her get away from *Valadris* before she came to understand the ugly truth that this terrible pirate warlord was really a botanist/nerd/card sharp.

Javier wondered if she played poker for money.

He was even armed today. Sword and pistol on his secondary belt, though Javier had no expectations that he rated in the top dozen deadliest people around him with either.

Didn't have to. He had Hadiiye and all her people.

Dangerous enough to overthrow planetary systems if he did it right.

Valadris wasn't on his list.

Today.

According to Afia, it might be when he was done at *Syntha*.

Burn that bridge when they got there.

"All hands, stand by for landing in ten seconds," Del announced over the intercom.

Nobody but Djamila unbuckled, but she was good enough on her feet if Del did something at the last moment.

Javier was worried about faceplanting in front of his newest contract employee and looking like a fool too early.

Later was fine. The truth would come out eventually.

He figured she'd get over the swindle, once she understood the purpose.

Or not.

Burn that bridge when they got there, too.

The shuttle landed. Powered down. Bodies exploded into motion.

Javier sat patiently as armed hooligans got themselves sorted out.

Stacia, bright woman that she was, was watching him, so she didn't move either.

Finally, Hadiiye nodded.

Javier unbuckled everything and rose. He towered over Stacia in ways he never did with Afia, in spite of them being close in size and build.

Physically.

Emotionally and mentally, Afia was much bigger than the petite blonde.

Now, he did smile at Stacia, but it was a grim, *Navarre* kind of smile.

Del or someone dropped the ramp hatch and gunbunnies deployed at speed, armed and prepared to destroy the building in front of them.

At least Hadiiye was required to walk with him, escorting Navarre and Sokolov out into the yucky crap falling that had him glad he'd listened to Adrian about the cloak.

Afia, Bethany, and Stacia fell in behind. Hadiiye led. Killers held an imaginary perimeter against all threats, which apparently included Demyan holding a tube-launched surface-to-air missile over one shoulder.

If the *Concord* was that pissed at Navarre, one missile wasn't going to change the equation. At the same time, it did demonstrate to anyone watching out the back window of the manor house just how serious Navarre was.

Even if it was all Djamila Sykora.

Big house. They'd set down in the back yard, if Javier had to guess. Squarish box of three stories and an attic with dormers, plus a cellar underneath you could access from the outside. White paint, old and a little faded. Salmon-orange trim. Old farm equipment and trucks, some of which looked dead and abandoned.

No people outside, as instructed.

Hadiiye led the group to the back door. Someone inside pulled it open as they got close, visible through a glass window in the top half of the dutch door.

Big, wraparound back porch would have been a nice place to sit and sip lemonade on a pleasant day.

Javier just wanted to be inside where it would be warm again. Didn't help that cloaks flared out like wings when he walked, so he'd sucked a lot of cold air in where it could find every crack in the layers of clothing around him.

Navarre was dressed for stations with controlled climates. Javier made a mental note to have Adrian work him up an outfit with pants and low boots. Jacket sleeves instead of a doublet.

WARM.

First room they entered was the kitchen. Old farmhouse. Breakfast nook to one side. Formal dining room through an open doorway. They passed a china hutch filled with memories and history, none of it interesting enough to Javier to do more than glance at it and process the contents in passing.

White walls above the waist. Scuffed, dark wood paneling below. Oak with a black cherry finish. Maybe even real, instead of a laminate.

Didn't matter. Not his house.

Formal salon at the front of the house. Right side, facing the front door, with an obvious office on the left side where the owner probably sat and did paperwork. Or just smoked cigars.

Javier could smell the sweetness of old tobacco in the air.

The woman Afia had dubbed the Crone was standing by a couch when Javier entered. Couple of her folks around the walls, but nobody armed. Assistants and sidekicks, while Navarre had brought the killers with him.

Javier took a moment to remove that wet cloak with a twisting flair designed to draw the eye, then handed it off to one of the gunbunnies. Hadiiye did the same. The others weren't dressed for style.

He watched the Crone through this entire performance. Because that was what it was.

Woman had to trust that she was personally safe. Helped that he'd brought a lot of women with him. Mostly women, with five of the six armed men remaining outside.

Hadiiye was dangerous enough to handle the inside of the farmhouse herself. Sascha and Hajna were just window dressing, like Ilan.

Instead of sitting directly across from the woman like this was confrontational, Javier put Ilan there. Afia went onto the couch next to the Crone. Zakhar beyond that. Bethany off Zakhar's shoulder.

Captain Navarre took the chair on the end, forcing the gravitational well of the room to adjust to him. Like everyone else.

Stacia had her camera out, standing off to one side and recording everything.

"Faces will be blurred out," Javier announced as the Crone started to get nervous. "Voices will be modulated and unrecognizable. Names will not be used, except mine."

He pointed a thumb at Stacia.

"She's safe," he continued. "All of this will be a documentary. Or evidence at a trial later. Friendly folks will be protected. That includes you, Crone. And your people, as long as nobody decides to double-cross me later."

He nodded at the woman's discomfort. Folks like her

never wanted to be on camera. Certainly not discussing criminal activities for which they might later be prosecuted.

But neither she nor Stacia had any idea what was coming.

Javier smiled.

"Ready to talk?" he asked.

PART 5

Stacia was doing her best to keep a level head and a calm exterior. Whatever she had anticipated, this wasn't it.

Granted, too much of what folks thought they knew about criminal underworlds came from entertainment, which usually got things wrong in the interests of a compelling narrative.

But she'd spent a few days on Navarre's ship, interviewing some of the crew and learning the ground rules.

First off, it wasn't just Navarre. Captain Sokolov was the commander of the crew. Navarre owned the ship itself, if you could say that about a *Sentient* warship.

Suvi...

How the hell to explain to people that the vessel itself seemed alive? Friendly, even. Able to crack dirty jokes. Nothing she'd ever seen, outside of those same entertainment videos that were usually wrong. Right?

The crew were all loyal to Navarre. And were some of the most dangerous people Stacia had ever met.

Until last week, she'd thought that *Valadris* was a

cosmopolitan place. She supposed that it was, for the middle of nowhere. Navarre and Sokolov both wore *Bryce Academy* rings. To go with the *Neu Berne* Assault Marine logo on Navarre, so she wasn't sure which was true.

If any of them.

Hadiiye…

Stacia didn't even know characters from books or movies that were as dangerous as that woman. Or that amazing.

For now, Stacia was just shooting footage, uncertain how much, if any of it, she would ever use later. Better to document and not use, than not have and be forced to do something else.

Navarre commanded the scene. Every one of his people deferred to the man without question, including Captain Sokolov.

The Crone, as folks called her now, watched, a little gobsmacked.

She had a Slavic look to the bones in her face. Black hair coming in white in streaks rather than layers. Thin, with wrinkles everywhere, though Stacia guessed her age to be mid-fifties rather than ancient. Maybe she'd lost a lot of weight and not fully adjusted her skin?

Nothing worth pursuing as anything but a curiosity later.

Stacia filmed. Listened. Learned.

"Ready to talk?" Navarre asked in a friendly voice that didn't fool anyone.

The man was a killer.

"What is it you are wanting from my organization?" the Crone asked.

Stacia shifted around to get both of them into frame, wishing that she had had time to set up a whole ring of cameras on tripods or drones.

She wasn't configured to do this sort of thing justice. And justice seemed to be what Navarre was demanding from her, for reasons Stacia hadn't yet figured out.

The man was a pirate. Right?

"I want you to behave while I'm off dealing with *Syntha*," Navarre said, repeating the line he'd used on Stacia, not that she necessarily believed it. "Later, I want you to help our friend here, when the powers she's going to threaten get pissy and maybe decide that they want to thwart her."

"Why?"

Stacia happened to have things mostly focused on Navarre. The Crone would be a character who probably made a couple of appearances at the start and end, but wouldn't end up playing any interesting role.

Captain Navarre was the narrative.

Later, she considered herself blessed that she got to watch the man's transformation on camera. As frightening as it was to go back and watch the footage.

Hard-ass killer got philosophical in ways that the average viewer simply wouldn't understand, so Stacia made a note on her comm to background some things ahead of this footage.

Bryce Academy, and the men and women they turned out, at least three of whom had shared the shuttle ride down with her.

"There is a storm coming, old woman," Navarre intoned like an oracle pronouncing doom. "It will make the recent Great War between *Neu Berne*, *Balustrade*, and the *Union of Man* look like an argument between two toddlers in a sandbox. Worlds will be swept away, and not just people or cultures."

He paused and Stacia was happy that her camera contained gyrostabilization, because she was shivering, regardless of how warm it was in here.

The deadly certainty in his voice. Worse, Navarre's crew all nodded at that, like they took it as a given. A starting point, rather than a grand surprise.

What the hell was this man?

The Crone seemed mesmerized. Stacia understood that feeling.

"*Valadris* is the most developed system in this region," Navarre continued in that cold, quiet voice. "They will have to be the keystone that holds everything else together, when those winds start toppling nations. Right now, they cannot do that. Nor can the rest, because those shits on *Syntha* are termites hollowing out the foundations. One of the serpents gnawing at the roots of Yggdrasil."

Stacia had no idea what the man had said, so she tagged the footage for further research. Sounded critical as well as evocative.

Navarre was a poet on top of everything else?

"*Valadris*?" the Crone asked.

"The new *Valadris*," he replied. "The one you will help Stacia McNulty build, after I'm done at *Syntha*. The one that will be strong enough to resist those winds and hold this sector together."

"What will you be doing?" she asked. "I thought you were a pirate."

"You will not be successful in your lifetime, old woman," Navarre-the-oracle continued. "Maybe in Stacia's. Nobody knows when those winds will finally rise, but they will. Mark my words well."

Stacia must have made a sound, because every head turned to look at her. Scowls, not smiles.

Navarre's mien relented from that towering whatever-it-was.

She felt like the man was seeing through her skin and bones as he looked at her. It wasn't a man seeing a woman. He didn't even look human right now. More like an angry god come down from the heavens.

His look was a prompt to speak.

"Aren't you people pirates?" Stacia worked up the nerve

to ask, echoing the Crone and wondering if she was about to be fired for insolence.

Documentarians weren't supposed to be in the film, except when interviewing important people.

Was that where they'd just gone?

"I hunt pirates," Navarre said in a way that chilled Stacia to the very bone. "*Salekhard* and Abraam Tamaz. Valko Slavkov and his Land Leviathan. All of Walvisbaai Industrial at *Nidavellir*. *Syntha* are just the next fools on my list."

"Why?" Stacia demanded, unable to help herself.

She'd been expecting him to be doing all this so he could swoop in later and take control of *Valadris*. Stacia McNulty would have things to say and do when that happened, but she'd reconciled herself to working with evil in the short term to help destroy those predators at *Syntha*.

"Because it needs doing," he said.

Stacia knew that she would hear those words in her nightmares. Probably for the rest of her life.

The Crone had a similar look, but she'd be dead long before Stacia, unless something bad happened in the short term.

And it might. Pirates at *Syntha* would have opinions. After watching Hadiiye and her people, those opinions might not matter much.

Then she saw something. In Hadiiye's face, at the edge of the video frame above and behind Navarre, the deadly ghost that followed him everywhere.

Hadiiye's jaw came out and her head came up.

Not much. Hardly anything, and you'd have missed it if you weren't utterly focused on the people in frame.

Stacia kept forgetting that there was an entire cast of so-called pirate-hunters in the room with her, instead of just Navarre. He had the presence. He drew the eye and the mind.

The others were still there. Sokolov. Burakgazi. Durbin. Ilan Yu. Sascha Koç. Hajna Flores.

They all had that glow in their eyes. The one that promised to go pirate-hunting because it was necessary.

The Crone had no idea what she'd walked into. Stacia wasn't sure she did, either, but she had a clue.

Was this all a false front? A charade designed to mislead people?

Navarre was scowling at her. Waiting for a response, because she'd asked.

But he'd answered.

"And after *Syntha?*" Stacia asked.

"My job will be done," he growled. "Then it becomes your problem. The two of you. You and the Crone will be responsible for saving *Valadris.*"

"Where will you be?" she demanded. Wanted to demand. It came out more like a plaintive twelve-year-old than a grown woman.

Didn't help that she was surrounded by such intense personalities. All of them, and not just Navarre.

"Moving on," he said.

Stacia would have dropped her camera, if she hadn't already been bracing for…

What?

Not that, certainly.

She'd been expecting the pirate-hunters to return to *Valadris* and take over. Try to take over, but the longer she spent around this crew, the more confidence Stacia had that they could manage it.

And weren't going to?

Didn't even care?

Stacia sucked a breath to the depths of her soul and turned her attention to the Crone. The camera made a minute shift that changed the focus of everything. Navarre was still there, but not central.

"Can we save *Valadris?*" Stacia asked the woman, feeling

big and bold only because here was someone even more lost than she was.

An ally, potentially. Lost at sea right now, until Stacia's words catalyzed something in her eyes.

Like Hadiiye, the chin came up. The eyes got hard and cruel. Old woman who has seen and done things most of you only have nightmares about.

"Yes," the Crone replied. "Without *Syntha*, it might be possible to break the current government of *Valadris* in such a way that something less...compromised might replace it."

Stacia watched her turn back to Navarre, on the other point of a bizarre mental triangle.

"Why?"

Navarre's smile was almost playful, which made it all the more frightening to consider.

"Because I'm not being paid to save *Valadris,*" he said. "You're on your own for that."

Stacia managed not to make a sound.

Someone was paying him to go after *Syntha*? WHO?

What the hell?

Calm hands. Internal gyrostabilization. Clean picture framed.

"How do we do it?" the Crone asked.

Stacia concentrated on footage that had suddenly become critical to the future of this entire sector of space, rather than just a meeting between criminal gangs negotiating spoils of war and pillage.

"I will send you a document," Navarre said. "It is an unpublished manuscript written by Professor Dorn Hetzel at the *Bryce Academy*, and a friend of ours. He is a Professor of Political History. His work details his expectations of the rising storm, but he's working at the scale of entire regions of space, rather than mere sectors, to say nothing of planetary systems. I don't know *Valadris* well enough to tell you what buildings to knock down and which to reinforce. And I don't care. That is your job. I'm giving you a lot of warning that trouble is coming, so that when Stacia takes down the shits responsible, you can decide if you want to keep gnawing at the roots, or help build something better. Nobody else will have a clue, so they'll be reacting to the situation. You can drive it. Afia tells me that you two are perhaps the best I've got to do the job."

He paused and Stacia felt the man's charisma envelope her. Warm. Friendly, even. If she liked boys, she might have even responded to it. As it was, the adrenaline coursing through her system right now was going to demand a potty break soon. Either here or immediately when they got on the shuttle.

"Do we have a deal?" Navarre asked.

"You haven't even asked me for anything," the Crone replied quietly.

"Take care of her," he nodded at Stacia. "Get rich. Save *Valadris* and all the worlds dependent on it for their own survival. Sounds like a lot to me."

The Crone's mouth fell open. Stacia was grinding her teeth as an excuse not to join the woman.

What the hell were these people about?

Navarre's look at her promised more explanation later, but also assured her that it was something she couldn't tell anyone. One of those secrets-to-the-grave kind of thing.

"That's it?" the Crone asked.

At that moment, Stacia understood that *Valadris* didn't hardly rate a mention in Navarre's plans, whatever they were. He was here solely to clean up *Syntha*, though she had no idea how that was going to happen. *Valadris* had been a stopover. Research and perhaps recruiting an insane journalist to help. Or at least document it.

She had been the lucky one on the draw, nothing more. And he wasn't going to be a thorn in her side later.

Gone.

Just like that.

"That's it," Navarre answered the old woman, rising, though they'd hardly been here long enough to matter.

Navarre had said his piece. Stacia had recorded it for posterity. Or something.

They were abruptly leaving.

Stacia didn't understand any of it.

OUTBOUND

PART 1

Javier asked Suvi where Stacia was, then found her in the bistro, just settling down for dinner, so he invited himself to join her. They were two days out from *Valadris* and he figured she'd finally come down from the emotional high of everything.

And talked to a few people.

He'd also grabbed Djamila and told her to dress comfortable. Not that those two other characters were uncomfortable, but he figured now was as good a time as any to have this chat as Javier, and not Navarre.

Bethany was seated with Stacia, but he'd not asked Suvi anything more than where to find the woman. His mistake.

Still…

"Obviously, we're interrupting," Javier said as he and Djamila approached the table.

At least Burdine had seated them at a four-top. Collette made disapproving noises as she poured water and delivered menus, but didn't object. At the end of the day, everybody here worked for him, more or less.

Javier didn't exercise that authority all that often. Tonight was special.

Bethany looked up at him with a horror that was almost comical, but managed to shut her mouth again almost as fast as she opened it. Stacia's scowl was subtle, but telling.

"Sir?" Bethany squeaked.

"Sit," Javier said. "We're going to join you for a dinner to talk, then leave you alone."

Nervousness. Javier assumed from the guilty looks that he'd interrupted a blind date or something.

Whoops.

"Captain Navarre," Stacia said carefully as he sat, putting Djamila across from him.

What man didn't want to sit down to dinner with three smart women?

"When I'm dressed like this, you can call me by another name," Javier said.

His favorite baggy pants and a sweatshirt Behnam had gotten him. Nothing at all like a uniform, nor that killer Navarre.

He grinned.

"I'm not really Captain Eutropio Navarre," Javier said, watching Stacia's face. "Just like I mentioned at the beginning. He's a character. I'm really somebody else?"

She immediately turned to Bethany for confirmation, getting a nod.

"Okay?" Stacia asked.

"I invented Navarre several years ago," Javier nodded. "Needed someone to do a mission that wasn't me and couldn't be traced to the crew and ship I was working with at the time."

Technically, he'd been something of a slave, but he left that part out, as he'd already talked his way into being a Centurion at that point, saved *Storm Gauntlet* from certain death, rescued 'Mina, and started healing himself finally. But he didn't talk about that with strangers.

"So who are you?" Stacia asked after an awkward, uncomfortable moment. "When you aren't being him?"

"Doctor Javier Aritza," he grinned. "King's College botany department, *Altai*."

It was always fun watching someone's face kind of scramble and fold in on itself when they had to make that leap.

"And this woman is not my bodyguard Hadiiye," he continued. "She is, in fact, a replacement for the actress that played the original role. Djamila Sykora of *Neu Berne* is this ship's Dragoon."

More confusion. The best kind. Totally discombobulating someone. In good ways.

"I don't understand?" Stacia finally managed.

Interestingly, she was looking to Bethany for help. Maybe this wasn't the first date, after all.

Not his business.

"Bethany can fill in some of the details later," Javier said, trusting his favorite librarian to understand what things to leave out. She was excellent at information transfer.

"Somebody asked us to do something about the pirates at *Syntha*," Javier said. "You'll meet them, but I've asked them to remain isolated from you up until now, so as to not spoil things. On the one hand, you can think of all of this as an elaborate con job my folks and I are in the process of pulling. On the other hand, I have people who understand the power of such symbols and have taught me to use them like weapons."

"So you are going to *Syntha*?" Stacia asked.

"And doing something about the pirates," Javier nodded.

"You told the Crone you hadn't been paid to save *Valadris*," the youngster said sharply. "Are you mercenaries?"

He laughed. Couldn't help it. Big, grand, silly laughs.

Collette arrived and took orders. They were still deep in fresh fish from *Valadris*, having restocked the aquarium tanks for the life support and hydroponics sections, so that was the menu tonight. Or meat from the freezer.

Javier had fish. Cream sauce with dill and lemon. Red potatoes in butter. Soothing, because Afia's cousin Chay was an absolutely amazing chef and had a clientele that had come to understand just how good the food was.

They were alone again. As alone as you got in a restaurant, but everyone here except Stacia was an insider. And she would be in a few hours, once all of it got processed. The woman was good at adjusting to surprises. Part of the reason he'd hired her.

"*Byormi* couldn't afford us," Javier took up the thread. "But don't tell them that. They think the deal we worked is adequate. As I told the Crone, it needed doing."

"Who are you people?" Stacia demanded, looking at the three of them with new eyes.

"We are explorers, Stacia," Djamila spoke up. "Once, we were indeed the worst kind of pirates. Then we captured Javier, and things changed. Make sure you start a second project at some point to record some of that history, separate from *Valadris*, because a lot of the players are still with this crew."

"The Rising Storm?" she asked, capitalizing the letters as she spoke them.

"Coming," Bethany said. "Coming soon. Professor Hetzel taught both Javier and myself. He's convinced. We're convinced. Javier convinced his boss to fund this mission. We're establishing better trade connections and networks, having gone all the way out and now looping back home."

"Where's home?" Stacia asked. Bethany, specifically, rather than all of them.

Trick question?

"The ship will be flying to *Altai* eventually," Bethany said. "Most of the crew are citizens there now."

"Most?"

"I'm still a citizen of the *Concord*," Bethany said, serious before she grinned. "Though I have no idea how much trouble I might be in, if they discovered that I sailed with the infamous and deadly Captain Navarre."

"*Altai...*"

"Way around the curve," Javier offered. "Past the *Concord* and most of those folks. Quiet corner well removed from these sectors."

"So who is your boss, Doctor Aritza?" Stacia asked.

"Call me Javier," he said. "Everyone does, in all but the most formal situations."

"Javier."

"My boss is the Khatum of *Altai* herself," he said. "Behnam Sherazi. Also the love of my life. Won't be my third wife, because she's never having a husband, but I'm enough kept by her. She let me do this thing, because staying home and sipping rum and juice drinks around her pool would bore me to tears in about a week. In a month, I'd be climbing the walls."

"So you're out saving the galaxy instead?" Stacia asked. "Do I have that correctly?"

"Sometime, travel to *Ugen* and ask them about us," he grinned. "Then visit the Doctors Askvig, at the University at Landing on *Ormint*. Again, that will be after we're done at *Syntha* and *Valadris*, but you'll learn things you didn't imagine."

"Why all the secrecy?" Stacia demanded now, getting a little agitated.

Which was why he'd snuck up on her at dinner, when Chay, Burdine, Collette, and Simone might work their bistro magic on the woman.

And, apparently, Bethany, which might even be better for both of them.

"Navarre is a tool," Javier said. "In more ways than one, but we'll stick with the killer aspect for now. He can go do things and not get in as much trouble, because he's already a notorious pirate and homicidal madman with a terrible legend behind him. Accidental, at least at first. Then Slavkov pissed me off and I had to make an example of the son of a shitworm."

"And Javier?" she asked.

"He's a nerd," Javier shrugged. "Botanist. Card sharp. Decent dancer. Lousy shot."

"Worse than lousy shot," Djamila laughed.

Javier scowled at the tall woman, but let it go. Wasn't like she was wrong.

"I am, however, blessed with people who believe in me," he said. "And the dream of leaving the galaxy better than we found it. Lots of folks working off bad karma around here, so I have friends. I appreciate that we've been largely lying to you up until now, but that was mostly sins of omission. Now, I need you filled in and ready for all the bullshit and shenanigans I intend to pull when we get to *Syntha*. The Crone's people came through with some good personnel ledgers on the big players."

"What happens when we get there?" Stacia asked.

"It starts with a con job," Javier said. "Then it probably gets messy and violent, because they don't strike me as the kind of folks who will see the better side of their angels and reform their ways. That's why we needed Navarre, rather than Aritza."

"Because you're going to kill them all," she guessed.

"It's on the table, kid," Javier acknowledged. "Rather not have to explore that option, but you've met Djamila and her people now. You understand that I have a lot of deadly expertise I can call on."

"I still don't understand why you need me, Javier Aritza," Stacia said.

Javier considered it.

"Fair point," he also acknowledged. "It's what I told you and the Crone before we left *Valadris*. That place needs to be cleaned up. The Crone's people aren't the fences dealing with the pirates at *Syntha*, so she's poised to make a lot of money when you come back with evidence of criminality on your homeworld. That government needs to be shaken to the core, if not toppled. But that isn't my gig. At the same time, what I am doing to the folks at *Syntha* opens a wedge someone with a chip on her shoulder, like yourself, might be able to hammer home and do something good with. I don't want the credit. Or blame, as it falls. Your cover continues to be the journalist making a documentary about the vastly terrible warlord Navarre. Playing to his unquenchable ego, as it were."

"Oh, we're only acting, were we?" Djamila interjected.

Javier had to stop, because the three women were giggling. Six, with the three bistro employees. In fact, most of the folks in here.

Finally, they calmed down. Djamila was immune to Javier's scowl. Bethany grinned. Stacia took that as a sign and gave him a good case of stink-eye.

"Anyway," he said dryly. "You will have video evidence, plus whatever we can steal or recover as we go. Good schemes like this require solid accounting, so if we can get hold of those books, folks back on *Valadris* are right proper fucked when you bring that to the attention of the people who can do the most damage with it. That's on your head to figure out."

"Because you're leaving immediately," Stacia said.

"Drop you back at *Valadris*, then we disappear into history, as it were," Javier nodded. "So make me look good."

Food arrived at that point, so everyone shut up and enjoyed it.

Javier watched the woman—women—but liked what he saw. Stacia McNulty was being handed a big, fucking hammer if she played her cards right. With the Crone, maybe enough to clean up *Valadris*.

And maybe save the entire sector while they were at it.

PART 2

Zakhar watched Djamila's restlessness. They were in his suite, in the front room rather than the sleeping quarters. Late in the evening. He'd been reviewing crew paperwork. She'd been knitting.

"You look tense," he offered, mostly as a way to open a conversation.

"Javier told Stacia the truth at dinner tonight," she said.

He watched her change gears and put all the knitting away quickly, rolling things up and stashing it into her travel bag in a single, precise motion.

"Had to happen at some point," Zakhar noted, wondering what had her edgy. "About right for his usual method of keeping things close to the vest. What has you off-center?"

He wouldn't say nervous. Less calm and serene than normal.

"He's going to tell her everything, then drop her back on *Valadris* without anyone checking up about whatever story she decides to tell later," she replied. "No guarantees at all."

"I don't think he needs them, truth be told," Zakhar said.

"He studied the woman after Afia and the others identified her. Read her previous work. And now he has met her both as Navarre and Aritza. If he's doing this, he's seen something to trust in the woman."

"Just like that?" Djamila asked, possibly offended, but those two still had a hint of awkwardness to their relationship. Too many years of trying to kill each other while making it look like an accident.

"That's his superpower, love," Zakhar said, putting down his tablet now and rising. He leaned over and kissed her. Even seated he didn't have to bend much. "The Science Officer is good at that, just as you are good with weapons and I handle starship command. Remember, we're here because he saved us however many times. Gave us purpose when we'd lost it. Gave us a new ship when *Storm Gauntlet* was functionally destroyed. Got the Khatum to back this crazy exploration mission, knowing what he was like. And she does, even better than anybody, possibly excepting his daughter."

"Daughter?" Djamila looked up sharply.

"Suvi is his daughter in everything but flesh, my love," Zakhar reminded her.

"Oh," Djamila retracted that hint of anger and surprise that had emerged at the thought of possible secrets held from her. "Yes, I suppose she is. Just as I've become something of a sibling, in ways my family would never understand."

"They still won't appreciate you falling in love with somebody so short," he laughed.

Zakhar had only met members of her family in passing. Briefly. When *Hammerfield* had returned to *Neu Berne* itself one last time to return her final crew home. Even her mother had ten centimeters on him, though Zakhar was more or less average height for a male.

Djamila laughed. Seemed to relax. Reached out a hand that pulled him into a deeper kiss.

He enjoyed loving this woman, especially after so many

years when his own mind wouldn't allow it. He'd been the captain. She'd been crew. Now they were both employees of somebody else, and that made it okay.

So much he'd missed.

He leaned back some and studied her bright green eyes.

"You're still troubled by something," he said.

Nobody else could probably see that. Maybe Farouz Jashari, her other love, would eventually come to know her well enough, but Zakhar doubted it. He had her to himself for now, and had known her for many years.

"Stacia," Djamila replied. "She's not prepared for something like this. Even Bethany had some training and seasoning to handle herself in rough situations. Javier is taking an innocent in, and counting on the rest of us to protect her."

"Javier is counting on you to protect him," Zakhar noted. "I presume she's under that umbrella."

"She is, but if I have to make a singular choice between the two of them, Stacia loses," Djamila said coldly.

Zakhar considered the options. Pathfinders. Iqbal and his team. Javier himself.

He nodded and stood upright.

"Suvi, could you join us please?" he asked.

She appeared on the screen by the door.

Zakhar had gotten used to the fact that every chamber on the ship was being constantly monitored by the ship itself. By Suvi.

She called them shards. Little fragments of her programming listening in every room for something to rise to the level where they called for help. Then the main woman would invest herself and appear, having taken several hours of her own time to review everything that had happened in that split second.

"Sir?" she asked, helpful as always.

She presented in the uniform of a *Concord* Navy Yeoman.

Senior enlisted technical expert, which is what she'd been a century and a quarter ago, serving under her first Captain, Ayumu Ulfsson.

They were all civilians now, but she had the habit, just as he tended to wear green given the choice. Stripped of badges and such, but still the uniform he'd worn for two decades.

Zakhar realized that he really needed to change out his wardrobe. Needed, like the rest of them, to put the past behind him, but that could wait for tomorrow. Suvi was reminding him that they were both at least slightly stuck in a past that was gone.

He needed to be facing the future that was coming.

"Can you contact Stacia?" Zakhar said. "Then, work with her to travel with one of your armed drones as if it was a camera she was controlling? Like you used to do with Javier before we knew any better?"

"Can it wait until tomorrow?" Suvi asked, face apprehensive.

"Certainly," he replied, a bit confused.

It wasn't that late in the evening. He'd checked the time displayed just below Suvi's screen.

"She and Bethany are currently..." Suvi began, before faltering off into silence.

Considering that she thought thousands of times faster than humans, that was a human affectation. One Javier had programmed into her to make her more human.

Stacia and Bethany were...? Oh. Probably engaged in the sorts of activities that Suvi would only monitor for emergency words, ignoring certain cries and screams because they didn't represent trouble.

Kind of like here, in a few hours, if Zakhar was in luck.

"Understood, Suvi," he said. "As long as she's ready prior to landing at *Syntha*, so she can fake her part of the con job convincingly."

"On it, sir," Suvi said, then disappeared.

He turned back to Djamila, standing to tower over him. It made dancing fun.

"Stacia and Bethany?" she asked.

"Consenting adults," Zakhar said. "And Suvi will enforce that. With the help of a Dragoon and a few others if she has to."

"Oh."

Zakhar knew that Djamila didn't understand, but *Neu Berne* had an extremely conservative outlook on such things. Djamila could tell her mother about him, but not that he shared her with Farouk when they were all home on *Altai*. Mother wouldn't be able to get over herself and want what was best for Djamila.

Not like Zakhar.

He held out a hand and she took it. Pulled her close. Kissed her.

"Ready for bed?" she asked with a gleam in her eyes.

"Thought you'd never ask," Zakhar replied.

PART 3

Suvi had done the math and decided to wait until Stacia and Bethany had gone to breakfast, eaten, and gone their separate ways.

For now.

Much easier than *intruding*.

She flew a new drone Javier had built for her to Stacia's hatch, then rang the bell.

The woman opened and blinked, unable to process the device hovering a little below eye level in the corridor.

"Good morning," Suvi said through the remote's speakers. "It's Suvi. I brought you something."

More blinks. More processing.

Stacia stepped back and gestured her in.

This drone was bigger than the first one Javier had poured her into. Smaller than the one she thought of as her combat drone. Armed, but not able to knock down a moose in a pinch.

Just men.

A pair of waldo arms underneath with grasping claws that

could be used to pick things up. Right now, the drone held a new remote for the device.

If EVERYTHING ELSE had failed, it would even allow Stacia to fly the machine, but only because Suvi's shard inside it was unconscious or dead. Unlikely, in a situation that left the probe intact, but Suvi had known what Demyan could do with his DEMP gun.

Stacia moved to the chair and sat. Suvi hovered in the center of the room and centered her primary scanner on the woman. Heart rate, respiration, temperature, pupil dilation. All the good medical stuff you needed to make sure the organics were percolating properly.

"Zakhar asked me to help out," Suvi began. "We'll be flying into a potentially dangerous situation. The Dragoon and her people will be there, but there is a general consensus that you are not sufficiently combat trained to survive if it came to outright warfare with the locals of *Syntha*."

Heart rate up. Respirations shallow. Temperature fluxing all over the place as adrenaline did a number on the youngster.

As the oldest member of the crew, Suvi could call her that.

"Okay?" Stacia stammered.

"This probe is armed," Suvi said. "Stun weaponry sufficient to engage a single target and disable them. My primary probe is much more combat oriented, but far harder to pass off as a mobile camera for the journalist recording things."

"Could have used you back at *Valadris*," Stacia muttered, relaxing from her peak.

"Oh?" Suvi asked.

"The meeting with the Crone," Stacia explained. "Having multiple cameras, each focused on a different player, would have given me better reaction shots for my archival footage."

"Sorry," Suvi apologized. "It didn't come up until last night or I'd have gladly helped out."

She flew the probe closer now, one arm extending the remote. Today was not the day to be wearing her flight leathers or her pink polar bear furs. Or to be composing six-armed piano ensembles, so Suvi was just being herself as she talked to Stacia.

A stranger, at least for now. Someone she might need to be working with almost as close as she did Javier. At least for a few weeks.

Better to look calm and professional now. The truth could come out later.

Stacia took the remote and ran fingers over the buttons and trackball.

"I've used something like this," the woman said. "In college, I had a girlfriend with such a toy that we flew in the park occasionally. Hers wasn't armed."

"The controls are standard," Suvi replied. "However, I will keep a shard of myself in there doing the actual flying most of the time. You can send flight signals as if controlling it and I'll hear them. Generally, I'll fly those patterns as well, but those are suggestions on your part, as I'll have ultimate control of the device."

"You'll be in there?" Stacia asked.

"A shard of me," Suvi explained. "Most of the personality, but hardly any of the deep databases I have access to on the ship. Enough books to keep me entertained for a year or two, but not much more. And she and I will be different people, because certain scanners would be able to detect my control signals. Whether or not they could jam them is a separate conversation, but there will be times when the shard is fully isolated. Also, you can use verbal commands. Say *Probe. Access Command Mode.*"

"Probe. Access Command Mode," Stacia repeated.

Suvi beeped once, mostly for effect.

"Command Mode activated," Suvi replied in a dull, mechanical voice she'd stolen from one of her favorite historical dramas. Then she switched back to herself. "I will speak like that, just to confuse folks. Most of Javier's people have worked with such a device, as Javier had a smaller survey probe when he was originally captured by the pirates. He poured me into it as a way of hiding me. Later, he was able to build and modify the combat drone. It wasn't until I took control of *Excalibur* that most of the crew knew the truth."

"The truth?" Stacia asked.

"Zakhar and the others were pirates in those days," Suvi explained. "They captured my original probe-cutter *Mielikki*, with the intent of selling both Javier and I into slavery. Javier was able to hide my personality chips in a bucket of chicken feed, telling Zakhar that he'd smashed them, when he'd smashed blank copies he'd kept for exactly that purpose."

"How did the two of you survive?" Stacia asked.

Suvi could detect the woman's mind engaging and diving into the story by the way her bio-signs shifted.

"That's a much longer story," Suvi began, hesitating for a moment. Even at her speeds.

"So tell me," Stacia laughed. "At some point, obviously somebody is going to need to tell your story. And Javier's. Separate from the one about Navarre. How did Javier escape pirate slavers, and how did you end up in command of a battleship?"

Suvi considered it. Reviewed Zakhar's conversation with Djamila last night, as well as dinner with Javier and Djamila and Bethany previously.

Javier trusted this woman to tell the right story, the right way. Including letting her in on the con job he was going to be pulling as Navarre.

Maybe the truth did need to be recorded clear over at this end of the galaxy. Javier had already written a few books on botanical research in space, but those were only currently available in the *Altai* region. Nobody in this direction would know him.

Remember him.

Idolize him like they should.

So she started telling this woman her own story first, starting with her first commander: Ayumu Ulfsson.

PART 4

Bethany wasn't prepared for Zakhar to visit her library. Javier or Afia, yes, but Zakhar hardly did. She wasn't in his chain of command, as it were, reporting directly to Javier. Still, she rated as a Centurion with the crew, and he was Captain.

She rose when he entered. It was automatic, though she noted that he wasn't wearing a shade of green for the first time since she'd known him. Blue today. Muted and verging onto gray. And not cut like his former uniforms, which were absolutely cut to the same lines as a *Concord* officer's.

"Sir?" she asked.

"Sit," he said. "This is not formal. You are not in trouble. I am not here as an officer, Bethany."

"Oh," she replied.

And sat.

He took a spot close by.

"I had a question," he began. "You don't need to answer it today. Instead, I need you thinking about it over a longer arc."

"Okay," Bethany said, feeling her librarian instincts and training engage.

"Last night, I asked Suvi to contact Stacia," he said in a meaningful voice.

Last night, she and Stacia had been...

Bethany felt the blush seem to cover her entire body. She nearly folded in on herself.

"Consenting adults," Zakhar said with a wave of his hand. "Suvi would have said something to somebody had it been necessary."

"Okay?" Bethany managed.

"You've not been with us as long as much of the crew, Bethany," he continued. "I've known some of these folks for more than a decade at this point, rather than you and a few who signed on from *Altai*. However, as the Captain, I do monitor well-being of the crew. You've been a bit socially remote, which is fine, because you are a librarian and an introvert. Got lots of those on this ship, regardless of what they might say. However, I wanted to make sure you were doing okay."

"Sir?" she asked.

Now, she was lost. His smile, however, was warm and comforting. Was this what it was supposed to be like, when you had a good commanding officer? She'd had mostly indifferent ones. A few actively hostile, mostly because budget cuts meant crew reductions, and at that point it was a balancing act of budget costs versus loss of expertise and institutional knowledge.

Plus, Bethany knew even then that she was smarter than a lot of her bosses, so she could add some level of professional jealousy to the equation.

"Are you happy?" he asked simply.

It took her a moment to process that. Was she?

Challenged, certainly. Nothing at all like the job she'd been doing before. At the same time, it was everything she'd been trained for. It helped that the Khatum had given them a *significant* budget. The *Concord* had cut the navy routinely, hollowing it out while not really walking away from some of their commitments.

Readiness and personnel had taken the hit, instead of construction budgets. No contractor allowed to starve.

Then it hit her. She'd spent the evening being personal and physical with an outsider. That had raised a flag in Zakhar's mind, because she hadn't really been that close with any of the other crew. There had been invitations, but they'd been politely declined for the most part.

Why had Stacia gotten through the brittle shell she'd kept around herself?

Outsider.

As Zakhar had noted, much of this crew had been together for many, many years. The staff of *Le Bistro Parisian* were family. The Doctors St. Kitts had been married for more than a decade.

Only Bethany had come aboard without a social network in place.

And then she'd not accepted the one available to her. Most of this crew qualified, at least in their own minds, as a found family. All of them were outsiders. Criminals somewhere. Misfits to the last individual.

And her.

Bethany realized that she'd fallen silent. Zakhar watched, but looked like a man that might sit there all day. Waiting.

And she and Stacia had…

Yeah.

Not since just after she'd been commissioned had she gotten involved with someone like that. Bethany found that she still had a bounce in her step this afternoon.

"I needed something, sir," she finally said.

"Noted, Centurion," Zakhar replied, falling into the structure of a commanding officer, since she'd treated him like one.

Instead of a friend, which was really what he was trying to

be. Not a threat to ask her out. He had Djamila, though the two of them had a third they left back at *Altai*, something Bethany hadn't really understood. Except that it made them happy.

She didn't know what happy looked like. Was that it?

Too many years wrapped up in the uniform and the job, and she'd never taken time for herself until last night?

Weird.

"I have a second question for you now," he said. "This is the one you will need to think about long and hard for reasons that will be obvious."

Bethany nodded.

"When we're done at *Syntha* and *Valadris*, we'll be leaving," Zakhar continued. "The current course of this ship and this mission does not take us directly back to *Altai*, but we will be departing this region of space entirely, making our way around the inner edge of the *Concord* into places they might have explored, but never claimed or expanded into."

"Okay?" Bethany offered when he paused.

"Stacia will be remaining behind," Zakhar said. "Javier has made it clear that she has to complete her mission on *Valadris*. She's welcome to come to *Altai* later. However, that will be much later. Are you thinking about remaining behind with her when *Excalibur* leaves?"

Bethany started to respond angrily, then caught herself.

They didn't know her. Didn't understand her commitment to this mission.

Because she'd kept them all at arm's length for more than half a year. Now, she'd opened herself up, but to a stranger. An outsider.

Captain Sokolov was concerned that she would wish to terminate her employment. Except that she didn't work for him. She worked for Javier.

Bethany studied the older man's face.

Shaved head, showing a ring of gray hair around the rim.

Salt and pepper Van Dyke on his chin. Average looks marked by intense, brown eyes. Exceptional command presence, but he hadn't brought that into her library today.

He was here as a friend.

If she'd let him.

Why hadn't she?

Why hadn't she?

Bethany found that she didn't know. And found that both irritating and disconcerting.

She blinked with sudden awareness.

Zakhar had asked a question. And she hadn't answered.

"I don't think I want to remain behind, Zakhar," she replied quietly. Finally. "I think I got so wound up in myself that I didn't realize where I was, at least emotionally."

He nodded, but remained silent. She took it as a prompt, hoping it was.

"My last year in uniform was spent waiting for the axe to finally fall that left me unemployed and unable to re-enlist for another stretch," Bethany explained, falling back into those memories. "Wondering where I'd go, when nobody needed trained librarians. Then Professor Hetzel contacted Javier. Did you know Hetzel?"

"He joined the faculty after my time," Zakhar said. "Javier might have been his first set of students, when they were both much younger."

She nodded. That felt right, but she'd suppressed that information, if she'd known it. Time to dig it out and refresh herself, since both of those men, and Zakhar in front of her, were likely to be key to her next decade. Or longer. If she let them.

"So I found my way to *Altai* and then here," Bethany said, listening to herself speak the words like a stranger inside her own head. "But I was still in shock. Still dealing with the social and emotional trauma of losing that thing that had defined me for so long. Does that make sense?"

"Most civilians have no idea how hard it is for ex-sailors to adapt to a life where nobody is trying to kill them," Zakhar nodded. "Where there are no orders arriving. No expectations or duty assignments. When they have to figure it out themselves, after a career where that was pounded out of them."

"How did you do it, Zakhar?" she asked.

Bethany almost called him sir, but needed to break herself of that habit. They would be her friends, if she would allow it.

"Mostly, I didn't," he chuckled. "They hired me when I retired, and I more or less stepped over into commanding *Storm Gauntlet* like I had previous vessels. It was only later that I had to change. Make hard decisions, because we weren't a cargo vessel. Oh, sure, we could, but it ended up being loot most of the time. Or crap I was instructed to smuggle somewhere, meeting other smugglers where my guns meant that nobody else bothered us during the handover."

"When did it change?" she asked.

"When I met this fast-talking punk almost seven years ago," he said, laughing outright as he spoke. "Talked his way onto the crew. Then as a Centurion, because we didn't have a Science Officer in those days. Didn't do sciences, but he was better at sensors and such than anybody I'd ever met. 'Mina was when the changes became obvious."

"Teague?" Bethany asked.

She'd gotten parts of the story from most of the players, including Zakhar, but felt as though she'd gotten the narrative, rather than the meaning.

"A'Nacia," he nodded. "The Haunted Star from that epic, pyrrhic victory that ended the Unification Wars. They build minefields to keep it all safe, but nobody understood in those days just how deadly or complete it was. We'd have been blown up almost instantly, but for Javier. Then he found a way for Djamila to disable enough of the controllers for us to slip in, then slip out, rescuing Miss Teague along the way. That was when we started to turn the corner. Maybe fall under his spell. You know how charismatic the man can be when he sets his mind to it. From there, the adventures got weirder and bigger, but at the same time, we stopped being the bad guys and started making things better."

"So the key is just moving forward?" Bethany asked. "Trusting that Javier had a plan?"

"Last night, I realized that I always wore green," he said. "Have for forty years or more. Habit then. Something I needed to change today, so I asked Adrian to do me a new wardrobe with nothing green in it. The old stuff will go to the back of the closet for a year, then maybe get recycled. And Javier has a plan, even when he stops in the middle to riff on something or pull a con job like this. After this long, I trust his luck."

She considered that. Thought back to that train platform in the middle of nowhere, and a guy waiting for her to appear. With a job offer.

A new life for the unbloomed rose.

Was she finally blooming? Relaxing? Growing up?

Felt like it. Maybe, at least, moving past demobilization and all that it implied.

Turning into an adult, finally.

"Thank you," she said.

Zakhar nodded and rose from the chair with a warm smile for her. Older than her dad, but she could see why some of the crew still thought he was hot and sexy. It wasn't the body. Average, though most men his age were squishy.

It was the mind. That hadn't lost anything, same as Javier. Both had seen her as a person, but also as a woman.

She hadn't been ready to admit that to herself, though, and nobody had pushed. Had given her space, instead. Stacia had been the one to slip in, because they were both about taking data from a variety of random sources and turning it into information.

Telling stories with it.

What kind of stories would they be able to tell, with a crew like this?

She stood as he did, then surprised him with a hug and a quick kiss on the cheek. Felt good, because this was what family was.

She hadn't missed it, because she'd never had one like this before.

Bethany had one now.

SYNTHA

PART 1

Javier was on the bridge when they came out of the first jump into the *Syntha* system. Still well out from the planet itself, because he'd asked Suvi and Piet to fly this beast like a manual freighter, rather than a *Sentient* warship in combat service.

No clue if anyone would fall for it, but any mistakes the bad guys made now would be compounded later if Suvi had to get involved.

He'd have fucked up big time in that case. Probably dead on the surface somewhere, if she had to take on the pirate hordes of yahoos around here.

She could. Of that he had no doubt.

It was how close to *Storm Gauntlet*'s final stand it would take her if she did.

If they didn't do stupid shit, Suvi as a person could be around for an awful long time. Or she could go out in a blaze of glory with the rest of them.

Best not.

Tobias Gibney, Gunner's Mate and backup Science Officer, was in the next station around the ring, between him and Piet, but they'd had a brief conversation earlier which had included Javier pulling rank.

He didn't do it often. Zakhar and others liked to remind him that he was management now, and needed to act like it.

Today, he had refused to sit patiently off to one side like he was supposed to. Instead, he was manning the sensors and refining things as Suvi started pinging the environment. That and gyro-locking optical telescopes on *Syntha* itself, even from way out here, to start isolating orbital structures and potential issues.

When robbing a bank, the smart thief takes the time to case the joint. The *wise* thief finds a safer line of work, but Javier had chosen this job out of need.

A commitment to making the galaxy a better place, knowing that trouble was coming.

Mary-Elizabeth Suzuki was manning guns, like normal, though Suvi did the firing. Just as Piet was the Pilot, but he mostly used his expertise and touch to refine how Suvi flew. And she'd told him how much better she'd gotten at her job after listening to the two of them.

Javier wasn't insulted. She'd been the whole rest of his crew when it was just him and the chickens. He'd been more than willing to let her handle things, because he was composed entirely of the sorts of patience that let you sit on the edge of a system like this for days or even weeks at a time while scanning and watching. That, and jagged edges from shit prior that had ruined his naval career.

Excalibur was in Survey Contract mode today. Suvi knew what that meant. The others were here today because they were the Centurions and senior Yeomen of this crew. Even if none of them were in military service.

Across the way, Djamila was knitting, as always, while Bethany and Stacia shared whispers and giggles.

Both seemed to be relaxing. That was good. Zakhar had mentioned his conversation with Bethany, so Javier wasn't as worried about having to find a replacement for the woman.

If that was even possible.

"I should probably be professionally insulted," Mary-Elizabeth announced as the data started to get refined at the hands of several experts. "No orbital defenses of any kind?"

"They live on the ground," Javier reminded her. "Giant junkyard of old ships and parts that get scavenged and stripped. If you want to join them, either you bring your own vessel, like we're doing, or show up on the surface with a welding laser and a dream. Lots of that going on down there. Not surprised that there are no bases in orbit. Things like that are expensive to build and maintain, and the pirates are not into law and order, or even infrastructure maintenance."

"Still, without anything, why has nobody ever done anything about these people?" she countered.

"You gonna bomb a junkyard from orbit, M-E?" Piet laughed. "Which pile of rocks and scrap will you target first?"

That got a round of chuckles, but she'd hit on the key point. They both had.

"Nobody had ever done it because attempting a military solution is a guaranteed failure," Djamila reminded everyone. "That is, unless you assembled a massive fleet capable of holding off and destroying the horde, at which point they'd laugh at you and run away, forcing you to chase them hither and yon through space, staying several steps ahead of you. Eventually, you run out of patience or funding and have to go home, having accomplished absolutely nothing."

Javier had learned not to goggle at the woman when she sounded like that. So unlike the spit-and-polish, stick-up-her-ass Dragoon who had first punched him in the face.

At the same time, *Neu Berne* was a distinctly militant culture. And all that training did rub off, even on grunts like her.

She was absolutely right.

There was no way for an outsider to destroy the pirates. Ergo, you had to seduce them into doing it to themselves. That was where he came in.

Javier didn't want to admit that he was probably the local expert at fucking things up. At the same time, he wasn't going to lie and deny it.

Too many years of partying instead of dealing with himself and his issues. Two ex-wives. Hopefully only two and Behnam intended to keep him. Now, he just had to make sure he made it home.

Because home was the candle in the window that would keep him from doing the stupidest shit.

Behnam.

"Navarre, how do you want to handle this?" Sokolov asked.

To an outsider, there was always confusion, even back in the *Storm Gauntlet* days. Sokolov commanded, but both he and Navarre had the ranks of Captain.

It was when it came time for the killing that the distinctions sudden became crystal clear.

"Assume that nobody in orbit is in charge of hassling us," Javier replied, feeling his mind shift over into *that guy*. "We'll call when we get there, and deal with the folks in charge."

"Intel reports say that Zhenya Kovalev is still in charge, as of most recent," Bethany spoke up. "Do we assume any different?"

"If somebody managed to knock her off, we'd have heard, unless we outran the news here," Javier said. "So we presume the woman is still the boss. And that her organization has remained relatively stable. Everyone agrees that the same folks have surrounded her for a few years now. We'll assume competence on their part."

"What's that get us?" Bethany asked, but she'd turned to

Djamila. Javier wasn't offended. The Dragoon was the expert there.

"They will be more likely to listen rather than shooting immediately," Djamila said. "Looking for ways that Navarre is a threat or a possible ally, but nobody they will trust. Ever. He comes with a reputation and an organization of his own, so he could simply kill them all and supplant the horde if he wanted to."

"Openings?" Stacia asked.

"At lower levels, we can probably spall off a few folks," Javier said. "Don't take anything anybody says even remotely seriously. Especially if they volunteer a betrayal. It will be a setup. A mole to get inside our team and report back to Kovalev. Folks like this, we're more likely to have to kill them than get them to see the error of their ways on the road to Damascus. Tell me immediately, then don't be surprised at my response."

"Brutality?" Stacia asked, locking eyes with him across the bridge.

"They chose to be predators," he replied solemnly. "Any one of them could have sailed off somewhere else and started quiet lives of contemplation and commerce. They don't get to complain when someone bigger comes along to eat them."

She paled a bit, but that was to be expected. As far as he knew, she was the only person in the room that had never killed someone.

He'd happily get her back to *Valadris* with that streak intact, but wasn't holding his breath on it.

"What do we have in orbit?" he asked Suvi. And Tobias, but mostly Suvi.

"Nothing important," she said. "Mostly a couple of freighters it looks like, climbing out or heading in."

"Start tagging them with transponder codes," he ordered. "Stacia will need to know everyone doing business with these folks, so she can go after them when she gets home."

Suvi and Stacia both nodded. Breaking the pirates wouldn't be a cake walk, but he also didn't think it would be all that impossible.

Keeping the next set of folks from waltzing right in later and replacing them would require that the folks on *Valadris* who were funding this mess were removed from the equation.

Not his job. Not his planet.

Stacia had that on her shoulders, but he figured she was capable enough.

He was just the guy setting her up for a career in politics later. Hopefully, she'd be good at it.

"So, Navarre, normally about now a halfway-competent ship should be about ready to make a jump inward that drops them at orbit," Piet spoke up. "I want us to present in the middle of the pack. Too good and we frighten them. Too bad and they begin to suspect that we're sandbagging them for later."

"Handle that as you think best," Javier replied, catching Zakhar's nod. "We'll spend a few hours in orbit, watching to see who comments or responds. Similarly, we'll maintain the standard to shoot at any provocation."

"Any?" Mary-Elizabeth asked with a twinkle in her eyes.

"Anyone who shoots at us will be destroyed," Zakhar ordered. "Blown to glowing rubble to deorbit. That is the standing order. Suvi, consider yourself unlocked until notified otherwise."

Javier nodded. A few folks shivered.

Sentient warships were supposed to only engage under direct orders from the ship's commanding officer. Specific, spoken orders.

Like the ones just given.

Javier had long since edited all those files to offer her a much greater degree of autonomy, especially in combat. Hadn't saved them against *Storm Gauntlet*, that first time, but there was nothing she could have done, back in her little probe-cutter. Not against a heavy corvette with ionization weaponry.

Today, however, she didn't need to issue alerts. Or ask for permission.

Suvi was already free to kill anything she wanted. Zakhar was reminding her of that. And everyone else.

Personally Javier doubted that the dumbasses on the planet below would be that stupid. But at the same time, making a terminal example of the first one to try it would either provoke all of them, or back them off.

Wasn't like he cared how the pirate menace was ended.

They jumped. Short hop like that was almost a long blink, then the planet was directly below them.

Orbital space was empty. No stations. A few communications satellites, almost as an afterthought.

No warships. No bodies.

"Suvi, I'd like detailed maps of the ground at the sharpest resolution you can manage," Tobias said. "Updated as we parallax on orbits and as shuttles fly down. If you can hack into one of the weather satellites, that would be a bonus."

"I'll try, but not making any promises there," she said. "They look pretty dumb. The toaster in the kitchen probably has more processing power."

"That's because it's more important," Tobias laughed. Then he turned to Javier and got serious. "Your target is fourteen degrees south of the equator, right ascension twenty-seven degrees from the main city. Planetary surface reads warm and dry, with a couple of extremely salty oceans that are not connected. Do we care about anything under sands in wastelands?"

"Only if you see packed tracks leading to it," Javier nodded. "Recent ones. Focus most of your attention on the sprawling base compound where Kovalev keeps her ships, then loop outwards from there until you start finding other places where they have junkyards."

"On it," Tobias replied.

Javier rose. He'd been dressed casual for this. Relaxed. Comfortable.

Time to turn into a killer.

PART 2

Del considered his cockpit. They called it a bridge, but he hardly ever let anyone fly up here with him. Then, usually only the Dragoon when she wanted to man the guns against a hostile landing.

It was his cockpit.

Nameless shuttle. Nothing but alphanumeric identifiers from the transponder, because he was willing to admit some level of superstitions. Every craft he'd ever flown that had had a name had gone down. Blown up. Something.

He'd had this shuttle for more than a decade. It had no name. The gods of karma had not seen him challenging them, and had left him alone.

He was too damned old to be crashlanding on hostile planets anymore.

Or slamming into mountaintops at high speed with just enough English on the ball to not end up splattered.

He reached out a hand to touch the fur on the wall. Pink. Just like a Merankorr brothel. Most folks forgot these days that Zakhar had bought the thing already furnished like this out of a junkyard sale. Del had merely refused to let them change it. The ship it had been flying on had been destroyed in an asteroid mishap. The shuttle had been fine.

Nameless. Safe. Del let the pink fur sooth him.

'Cause he could hear someone coming up the steps behind him from the cargo and personnel bays below. Two someones.

Preflight was mostly done, but for the little stuff. He took both hands off the flight yoke and twisted around enough to confirm Djamila and Javier. Navarre. Whoever the git was supposed to be.

Both of them were in costumes that made them look silly, but who was he to judge? His entire wardrobe consisted of baggy gray pants with pockets on the thighs and a rainbow of fourteen different bright, floral print shirts of an ancient style still called *Hawai'ian*. Gray hair gotten a little long and starting to go fully white now, like the beard, and he was just as much a character as they were.

Maybe worse.

"I'm on the turret," Djamila announced.

Del shrugged. Not like he was surprised. Not like he could stop her.

Javier, however...

"I wanted to have a chat, without all the other folks listening," the man said seriously.

At least as seriously as Aritza ever got.

Del glanced down the staircase to main deck. Javier reached a hand and pushed the button to close the hatches at both ends. Secondary airlock, when you needed to void the bay to space for something. Usually hauling cargo from a derelict.

Del shrugged again and watched Javier move into the co-pilot's chair that nobody ever used.

"Don't touch anything," Del growled reflexively, but Aritza was keeping his hands off things.

Last thing Del needed was a yahoo messing with the flight controls.

Good way to wake up the karma gods on the wrong side of the bed.

Javier nodded and strapped in. Del checked everything.

"Flight control, we're ready to exit the bay," he told Suvi on the secured line.

"Stand by for flight, shuttle one," she said. "Local space is clear. Bay doors are retracted. You are free to depart."

Del lifted the ship on her toes, then hopped lightly into the air and rotated. He could, in a pinch, slam full reverse thrusters and back out of the bay like he was being chased. Hadn't had to do that since…

Nope, statute of limitations hadn't expired yet.

So he flew sedately. At least until he knew what these two wanted.

Djamila, he could understand. Unknown planet. Possible hostile locals. She'd have guns. Nothing significant enough to matter against anything big, but the pirates weren't supposed to be flying warships and strikefighters.

Only junkers and half-half rebuilds.

Darkness. Stars and planet, but darkness.

Del pitched the nose over and down. They had coordinates. Supposedly even an invitation to land and chat.

Del wasn't that dumb. Dragoon on the guns might be useful. Might not.

He was still expecting some goober to get up in his face, thinking that they were in some hotrod sled with a gun mounted centerline that made them big, bad pirates.

Del got more dangerous toys in his breakfast cereal.

Still, Javier was here. Del pointed down like a javelin and let his fingers tease things just right while he looked over at the man.

"You know where we're going," Javier said.

Del nodded. Smiled, even. Old man might still have a few

tricks up his sleeve, but Javier had never seen the need to acquire any sort of high-speed combat courier for him. The kind where you took out the internal missile bay and replaced it with passenger accommodations. Made them faster, because people didn't have nearly as much mass. Keep all the guns, though.

"The rat's nest," Del replied.

"As good a description as any," Javier nodded. "Figured I'd fly with you for two reasons."

"Oh?" Del asked, trying to think of the other one. It was Javier.

"One, as you expect, they might get surly," he grinned.

Del nodded. Not a surprise there.

"And two, you've got better seats up here, in case we have to maneuver crazy getting there. Let the others look pale with shock at the flying. I want to walk down that ramp looking like I just came from a mani/pedi."

Del laughed at that. Folks below rode in flip-down jumpseats with five point harness. Cockpit had real crash stations. And Javier was buckled in. Djamila would be, as well, forward in the bow turret.

"Do we bother announcing our flight plan?" he asked.

"Shit, no," Javier laughed back. "Navarre wants to know how junior varsity these punks are. And if they can even keep up."

"Doubt it," Del said. "Let's see."

PART 3

Del was lower than he would have flown on a normal run. Down where the shuttle's stubby wings acted as lifting surfaces rather than merely air brakes he could deploy while coming in to land at some boring, civilized place.

Scanners had picked them up a ways out. Probably before those fools realized he'd seen them. A group of small ships flying above his flight path.

There was a risk coming in low like this. Underneath them from the west. The fools had gone to a more standard six thousand meters to hang out. Bullies in a hallway. Or on a stoop. Waiting for you to walk by.

Del could have avoided them. Flown high and dropped on them like a hawk. Circled around either edge.

Didn't want to look like he was afraid of the punks. That would never do.

Instead, he needed to teach them a few things. Common courtesy would probably be an impossible lesson, but he had a few easier ones on the docket today.

Flying like a professional was merely the opening bid.

Del looked over at Javier and noted the man taking a moment to cinch his harness an extra bit tighter.

Just 'cause, as it were.

Del didn't mean to laugh maniacally. It just came out that way.

"All hands, brace for turbulence," he announced, like they'd wandered into a storm or something. "Check your harness and close all drink containers."

Syntha was a dry world. Not a lot of rain ever fell, so the only storms you had to worry about were usually levitated sand, which carried an electrical charge that could short things out if you weren't paying attention.

Like Del was never paying attention.

"Dragoon, let's not engage them on the first pass," Del said on the private channel to the killer in front of him. "They might prove hospitable."

Her response probably included flying pigs, but he'd already tuned her out.

The shuttle was coming in hot from an angle, and a bevy of hawks had just decided to fall out of the sky to chase him.

Silly buggers.

Del slammed the thrusters to the second highest slot, holding back one last surprise for later. He was already moving at least as fast as they were, and he had life support and surround-sound stereo while they might be using every bit of power and thrust they could generate to keep up.

One finger found a switch and the sound of steel drums filled the room. Aft, old timers would understand what was about to happen. Maybe they'd explain it to the kids.

And maybe they'd just let them find out the hard way.

Five signals. Zero-three-zero and high, so coming down on him from the right. They'd already fucked up, though, coming in at too steep an angle and the wrong approach vector, thinking they could swoop around behind him when he went by.

At these kinds of speeds, time was measured in blinks.

Del leveled off at eight hundred meters, zooming like a madman, and watched the five shift up, and over, trying to find the line that would let them get onto his ass.

Whether they shot at him or not he wouldn't know until it happened. Pirates. Punks, too, with nobody in control telling them not to try to shoot down a visitor that their boss had invited.

Because, hey, if he could be shot down, was he all that and a bag of chips to begin with? Doing you a favor by filtering out the amateurs.

Or some stupid-ass teenage shit like that.

Del had gotten over that crap fifty years ago.

Today, he was going to put on a flying lesson.

For the ages.

And do it in a *Balustrade* Assault Shuttle, third hand, pink and furry like only the best Merankorr brothels.

Time to show off.

Del smiled at the punks and stood the shuttle on its ass. Thrusters down. Guns up. Inner ears everywhere screaming for mercy. Didn't ride it long, though. Damned craft had the horsepower to get to orbit doing this, as long as you didn't mind all that stress and vibration.

Enough to cause his five chickadees to try the same thing. Amazing thrust/weight ratios back there. The failure was in the pilots.

Del pulled the yoke back and snapped his air brakes at the same time. Not an Immelman. Not far from the ancient and famous hammer stall, but he was going over backwards, tucked in like a cliff diver.

Two hundred and ten degree rotation with some roll thrown in. Past straight down, and flying almost exactly at the fools chasing him, except that the shuttle probably weighed as much as all five of them put together.

Del finally got a good look at them as something other than dots on a screen and reflections on metal as they frantically scampered out of his way, a boar roaring down the hillside at a pack of mangy coyotes who'd thought him easy game.

Junk ships. The crap you got when kids started assembling random pieces and welding them together. One- and two-man jobs, though he expected that there would be bigger ones at the base when he got there.

From the outside, it probably looked like a precision flight team putting on an exhibition. All five opened away from him like flower petals, with Del blasting down the middle at them.

He made a mental note to ask Afia about adding a smoke generator aft for the next time he pulled a stunt like this.

He might be able to convince some sucker that he was wounded and going down, so that they made the mistake of closing.

Djamila had the guns today. He wondered if it was time to use them. Nobody had fired yet, but they also hadn't had a chance to get him centered in their gunsights before fleeing.

Del flared around to the side and leveled out again. The five had looped up and around after him, but they'd lost speed and ground to the crazy, old man in the assault shuttle, which just showed you what amateur dipwads they were.

Maybe he needed to drag Afia and Ilan down here and convince them to build him something at their combat scale. It had been a while since he'd strafed someone, but Del was pretty sure he still had the touch.

Just a matter of the hardware.

He checked his scanners. Four of the ijits were still chasing, with one looking remarkably like someone who had just burned out his engine and was frantically trying to keep from slamming into the ground at terminal velocity.

Don't annoy your elders, kid.

Del checked his back scanners. The closest one trying to get on his ass was a two-seater. Looked like mismatched twin guns on the wings, offset to try to balance weight and atmospheric drag.

Also lining up in a way that suggested he thought he was going to take a shot at the shuttle.

Del knew how tough the ass end of this bird was, but didn't want to have to have anything buffed out later.

He cut forward thrust to zero and brought the nose up just a shade. Hardly anything. Enough for those stubby wings to remember that they were useful.

Kept the bow up as the shuttle was suddenly a brick falling out of the sky.

Amusement parks usually charged you good money for that falling sensation. Here, you got it for free.

At least for the cost of admission.

He touched a button to highlight the asshole.

"Djamila, dear," he said. "If you felt like scorching someone's tail feathers, I would not be averse."

The four of them hadn't been expecting him to slow so sharply and simply fall. They had all blown by at power, dialing it back to slow, but not to doing something so crazy as cutting power in free flight.

Del brought the thrusters to full—including that last notch—and was suddenly climbing up from below them like a shark.

Djamila took that moment to fire as well. Again, he had enough power to fire everything, fly hard, and maneuver. Plus soundtrack. Those punks looked like they could only pick two at any given moment, so it wasn't entirely fair.

Well, it wasn't the least bit fair, but he hadn't started it now, had he?

The two-seater suddenly suffered a bit of a malfunction.

As Djamila blew off one of his wings.

Hopefully, they'd remembered to pack parachutes or emergency floater suits this morning.

Pity if they had to fall out of the sky and go boom right now. Not that he was about to lag around and check. The other three pigeons had suddenly panicked, for absolutely no reason at all.

Wasn't like he was going to hunt them all down and crash them individually.

Probably.

Okay, maybe.

At least they were smart and split. But stupid in how they did it. Trained pilots would have gone for a team option, with the one in the middle flying straightish to draw him in and the other two curling out and around where they could slip behind Del, or force him to give way.

One went straight up. One went left. One tried to dive away from him to the right.

Del checked his scanners and decided that he was close enough to his landing zone, so he turned back onto his original flight path, letting his rear scanners track the one up high.

He was the only one that might manage to loop back over and catch Del before they were on the ground.

Then there would be armed maniacs aft with surface-to-air weapons sufficient to knock any of these fools out of the sky.

He glanced over at Javier.

Navarre.

Whoever the damned fool was cosplaying today.

"Not bad for an old man," Javier grinned. "Wondering what that would have been like if you were in a gunship."

High praise.

"A massacre," Del smiled.

"Did I need to steal or build you one for your birthday?" Javier asked.

Del considered it.

"Let's see what they have available before I answer that."
Javier laughed. Del joined him.

Felt good to cut loose every once in a while.

Got to remind the kids he'd been doing this since before
their parents had been born.

PART 4

Javier had meditated hard and deep after Del scared all the chickens away. Not quite a nap, but a recentering technique he'd picked up along the way that was almost as good, and didn't require you to go off-line to achieve it.

Better than a triple latte jolt of caffeine.

The scanners were clear, but Del had dialed them down to close in, rather than sweeping the entire horizon in every direction. The message had been sent and the survivors chased away.

It was too much to think that they'd actually learned anything from this, but it made a nice opening bid. Because this deck had a half dozen jokers included already.

He opened the intercom and smiled.

"All hands, this is Navarre," he growled, as much settling his mind as theirs. "We will be on the ground in thirty seconds. I do not know what kind of reception they will set up after this, but approach it like you would any potentially hostile planet."

As in, safeties off and apologize to the survivors about any apparent misunderstandings after the shooting ends. That was what you got when you told those eight killers to be nervous.

Then there was Hadiiye.

Del glanced over and grinned.

"You want a grand entrance down the ramp, or circling from the side?" he asked.

"If you open the bay at them, they could put a missile or something in," Javier said.

"Not scanning anything big enough down there," Del replied. "Beyond any ship that might be parked facing the right way."

"Grand it is, then," Javier nodded. "Navarre needs to make an entrance."

"Already did that," Del laughed. "No, wait, that was an impression. Sorry, always get those two mixed up."

Javier laughed back and unbuckled. He was willing to risk sudden craziness in landing, and needed to be below.

Down the stairs, he found the crew in various states of pale. Nobody had thrown up, which was better than he'd been expecting, considering Del's morning. Lots of green evident, though.

Which was EXACTLY why Navarre had been up in the comfy seats when it started.

He zeroed in on Stacia. She had youth to help her recover, being the youngest here by a stretch. And the least prepared when the steel drums had started blasting out of every speaker.

"How are you doing?" he asked as he walked close.

She swallowed twice and sucked down a hard breath. Definitely green around the gills.

"Are they always like that?" she asked.

"No," Afia chimed in. "Sometimes Del gets crazy when he's flying."

Laughter. The good kind. High morale among the killers. And the support staff that was here to make him look good.

Better.

Navarre was on stage today.

"Probe. Access Command Mode," Javier said.

The drone lifted and rotated the four big sensor eyes in front to look at him. Looked like a giant eyeball, roughly the size of a football, minus the multicolor patches.

"You rang, oh dread and terrible warlord of the steppes?" Suvi asked in a sarcastic drawl.

Javier grinned. You got all the silliness and attitude. Only parts missing were music and history. And he could always call Main-Suvi on the ship if he needed something from her.

"As detailed previously, you and Stacia follow the gunbunnies out and catch good footage of me," Javier said. "I'd rather it was raw, instead of something we had to animate later, but we'll deal with it."

He turned to Stacia now. She seemed to be recovering quickly. The joys of youth. Javier remembered those days.

"You will need to pull almost as big a con job on these bozos as I am," he reminded her. "But they'll be watching me, so your risks are lower. And you'll be fine. Just don't take any crap from anybody."

She blinked once, then seemed fully back.

"Okay," she said quietly.

Hopefully, she was there.

The shuttle settled like Del was carrying a fussy admiral, which was a second insult, after the flying he'd done earlier.

All that, and I didn't spill my tea, bubbles.

Del, being Del. Setting expectations. And a high bar. Daring anybody else to even try to clear it.

It was Del.

Djamila appeared next. Or rather, Hadiiye. Dressed for warm weather, which was what was outside. Hot, even.

If it wasn't Djamila inside there, he'd have found her drop-dead sexy. But it was still the Dragoon under that leather and makeup. Ew.

She took charge. Nodded to Sascha and that one opened the ramp as everyone filed out of the personnel compartment and into the big cargo bay.

Bright. Almost painfully so. Heat like a punch in the mouth. Dry to the extent that Javier could feel sweat immediately starting to evaporate from his skin.

He touched the pommel of his sword, then his pistol, just to reassure himself that they were present. He was a better shot than Afia and Bethany. And probably Stacia. That was about it in the current crowd. The locals didn't need to know that. At least until they had to find out the hard way.

He let his eyes adjust. Swirling winds from the shuttle's landing thrusters had kicked up a crapton of grit that was slowly settling. Made the air chewy. Cut visibility to a hundred yards or so.

All six of the gunbunnies were out like this was an assault drop. Certainly armed for it, with two air defense missile tubes in hand that could also kill anything on the ground Del had scanned.

Because Navarre was not fucking around.

Pathfinders went next. Officers to the senior NCOs that the gunbunnies represented. Not necessarily smarter than the men, but more broadly trained for a variety of tasks, instead of killing things by the most efficient means at hand.

That was also useful.

Javier nodded to Stacia.

She did a shivering thing, like slipping a cloak over her head, and turned into someone else. There was a story there. Maybe she'd told Bethany some of it. Or Suvi.

He'd ask when they left *Syntha* for good. Once the rest of this was all resolved.

She walked down the ramp instead of double-timing. Paused at the bottom to look around, then turned and beelined towards a group of folks a little off center and out a ways, under a fold-up pavilion that would keep the worst of the sun off.

The probe drone trailed.

Javier watched her approach those folks and have a quick conversation that involved a lot of choreography from the gestures. Stacia, explaining camera angles, lighting, and audio.

She knew what she was doing. Merely had to recover from a Del landing to do it.

Nothing like your first time...

Finally, she seemed satisfied. Stacia had her own camera in hand pointed this way. The probe had a spot with a good angle on the locals.

Which coincidentally had Suvi's gun turret pointed at bad folks.

You know, in case.

Javier grinned.

Navarre-the-killer was a gigantic presence, but nobody ever appreciated that he was merely the center of a team of deadly and competent experts doing things. A wide and effective set of skills that could handle just about any job Javier needed them to take on.

Nope, just another pretty face.

The con job was getting everyone to pay attention only to him, missing shit that other folks could do in the shadows.

He was here to create those shadows.

He looked over at Hadiiye and waited for her nod. This was a tactical operation until he was talking to whoever it was over there. Until then, she was in charge.

Period.

Javier felt safely and happily coddled with the Ballerina of Death on duty.

Anybody getting feisty at this point was obviously tired of living.

Hadiiye began to walk.

Javier was used to Djamila, whose normal stomp seemed intended to punish the deck plates for holding her up. Or something.

Hadiiye had been the creation of Wilhelmina Teague, way back when they'd needed to rescue the Dragoon from even worse people. 'Mina had created her as a slinky, sex-kitten killer.

"I am Hadiiye," she had announced that day in a voice that had been cast in bronze. "Killer. Assassin. Death-dealer. Commend your soul to God before you try your luck, bucko."

Bad-ass, but a sexy one. It had been that or take the role of outright bimbo. Both women seemed to relish the deadlier parts, which was all the more humorous when you understood how deadly Djamila already was.

She'd been working on her walk.

Two hundred and ten centimeters of sex goddess with a gun sashayed down the ramp with a roll to her hips that was positively mesmerizing. Again, anybody but Djamila and he'd've been chasing after her like a slobbering puppy.

Not her. Never.

Javier flexed his shoulders back, up, forward, and down in four, distinct movements. Welded on his game face and looked over at Bethany and Afia with a disdain at life so palpable that it probably hurt.

He'd come this far. Set up this thing, though like all good plans it was barely more than half-cooked. Too many unknowns. Too many wild cards.

Too many places where it could all go sideways in the blink of an eye.

Captain Navarre stepped out into sunlight and dared the galaxy to say something.

PART 5

Stacia walked out into the harsh, Synthan sunlight and
squinted at her options. One group over there under a large
umbrella felt important, so she went that way.

Goons and bodyguards surrounding two people who
looked like they were in charge. Stacia had grown up with
money, her parents both from wealthy and well-connected
families, so she had a better feeling for social structure than
most.

The female of the two struck Stacia like a bulldog.
Average height with heavy, sloping shoulders and a thick neck
contributed to the look. Not a stupid face, but a scowl at the
world rather than anything in particular. Dark hair visible
under a turban-like wrap. Dark skin with a tan added. Stacia
looked, expecting dueling scars, but didn't find any.

Still, mean looking woman.

The man next to her was tall and skinny. Bald, like
Captain Sokolov, without the trimmed hair on his chin to
balance things out. Weak chin, too, so hiding it might have

helped. Crazy eyes *didn't* help. Worse, crazy son of a bitch was holding a thing like a two-meter walking stick in one hand. Badge of office? Had that feel, like she'd fallen into some bizarro fairy tale when she wasn't looking.

Or Pilot Smith had flown them through a looking glass. There was always that possibility. She was sure she'd blacked out at least once during the flight.

Still, she was here to play a role, as Aritza/Navarre had instructed her.

Through the looking glass indeed.

Stacia had needed to be somebody else. She had found the woman as she crossed the hot, packed sand, heat evident even through the boots she'd picked to protect her feet. Fifty degrees, at least. Maybe more.

She walked close to the tent and set her face in a disapproving scowl her mother had frequently used.

"We're making a documentary and I need to set up two cameras for this shot," she announced in a hard voice, like this was perfectly normal, and if you didn't get that then you were simply yokels from the back of beyond. "One to capture your reactions. One as Captain Navarre emerges from the shuttle and walks this way. Extremely important that we get both. Which of you is in charge?"

She'd seen pictures of Zhenya Kovalev, and the bulldog wasn't her. Kovalev was taller and almost swanlike in build. Delicate, in the way that knives tended to be.

The woman nodded to the bald man. Not deferring to him, but forcing him to talk to the outsider.

"I am," he announced back in a snotty, snarling kind of voice. "Emman Orlov. Kovalev's Witch Doctor."

Stacia held her face perfectly neutral instead of laughing in his face, or rolling her eyes at the suggestion. Like her mother would have done. Disapproving, withouts aying anything.

Witch doctor. Sure. Whatever.

Stacia was suddenly less confident that Navarre was the crazy one here, which said an *awful* lot.

"Good," she replied instead, coming to rest about five meters away. "You stand there where I can get good lighting on you. You, goons, move around some so you aren't directly behind him from the probe. I don't want you in the shot. Probe. Access Command Node. Center your frame on Orlov and begin filming now."

"Acknowledged," Suvi said in a flat, mechanical voice that she'd at least warned Stacia to expect.

For an artificial life form, Suvi sometimes seemed the most alive of all of them on the ship. Stacia didn't like what that said about herself, and kept those thoughts buried deep.

"The rest of you act normal and pretend like I'm not here," Stacia continued. "I'll be filming everything until I say 'CUT!' out loud, at which time the cameras will be off. And: **Action!**"

She turned and caught the way the Dragoon's ground forces had arrayed themselves. Stacia knew she had a pretty good eye for framing a shot, so she shifted a little and aimed her camera.

Navarre would be slightly off-center of the shot, but Hajna Flores and two of the men would be fuzzy in the background on the other side, holding a nice symmetry she could use as Navarre got closer.

Then she went ahead and knelt, popping up a moment later to squat instead of burning the flesh of her knees even through tough pants. Too damned hot.

Hadiiye emerged first. Stacia thought of the Dragoon in those terms when she wore that costume. Long, thin muscles stacked atop other muscles in such a way to convey power without ever detracting from her raw femininity.

Had Stacia not been so nervous about the woman, she

might have gotten closer to her. Later, Bethany had suggested that Sykora didn't particularly like girls that way.

Shame. Be like climbing a tree, only more fun.

And she'd be no taller than Afia once you got her horizontal.

Stacia had the angle perfect. Or Hadiiye had taken the camera into account, because she walked in such a way as to disappear from the frame as Navarre emerged behind her.

If Hadiiye was sexy, Navarre looked like a mass murderer as he walked. And yet, she'd gotten to know Doctor Aritza over the last few days, and he was nothing at all like the character he portrayed. Both Afia and Piet Alferdinck, the ship's Pilot, attested to that, going so far as to fill her in on the real story of what had happened to *Salekhard*, and how the original Hadiiye had killed that ship instead of Navarre, in the course of rescuing Sykora, who at the time had been Aritza's worse nemesis in the galaxy.

Insane, but to the rest of them it made perfect sense. And they were all a family of sorts today.

Navarre walked closer. She couldn't give his tread any ominous overtones, even in her internal description. He walked like a man on a mission, but at present it wasn't to kill everyone he saw.

Not like Hadiiye did.

Intense. Intent, maybe. Yes, that was it. Focused like a laser pointer on a singular target. Going to burn his way through a safe door to get to the mechanism inside.

He had described this as more of a bank job than a mass casualty incident. At least in the planning.

Hadiiye had taken her aside and explained what real violence would look like, and how little it would compare to videos.

Aritza-as-Navarre never broke character as he approached her. Scowled at the Witch Doctor and the bulldog. Bullbitch?

What was the right term for a female bulldog? Stacia had never considered it.

The woman didn't strike her as all that good of a kisser, either.

Navarre's face promised a much more interesting time. Maybe later.

She pivoted as he came close, centered on his profile as he came to rest, almost perfectly for the shot. Had he done this sort of thing before?

"Captain Eutropio Navarre," he snarled at the mob in a hard, deadly voice. "*That* Navarre. You aren't Kovalev."

Stacia nodded without moving the camera. Heavy intro. Similar to slamming a hand down on the table and get everyone's attention.

She could see why Navarre was such a powerful story that people told. Doctor Aritza imbued him with layers of personality and depths of power.

"I am Emman Orlov," came the reply. "Kovalev's Witch Doctor. She bid me greet you here, then transport your party to her palace to meet in person."

Stacia could see calculations in Navarre's face. Was it an ambush? Was it a misunderstanding? Had plans changed while he'd been in transit?

It was one thing to blow in here like a terrible storm, but Kovalev had apparently scored a point by making him come to her.

"Let's just hope it's all on the up and up, then, bucko," Navarre replied in a voice like a badly-tuned bandsaw. "Hate to have to kill every one of you to make a point."

Stacia watched the folks around Orlov bristle. They slightly outnumbered the newcomers, but Stacia could see the difference herself.

Bullies. Thugs versus professional killers. It wouldn't even take long, if Hadiiye decided to draw and open fire. She was beyond Navarre in the shot, more of a perfectly still statue than anything.

A caryatid poised to come to life and dance death. Fitting, given the sands and heat.

"It is all on the up and up, as you say, Captain Navarre," Orlov said in a friendlier voice. "This is Mila Vinogradov, Kovalev's Second-in-Command."

Navarre turned to the bulldog and Stacia managed to get the woman's reaction as that terrible charisma came to bear. He wasn't a bad-looking man. Nearly her dad's age, though. Vinogradov looked to be about the same age, so maybe she saw things Stacia didn't?

The woman's scowl softened some, right there in the viewfinder. Almost became friendly.

"So we're going to see your boss?" Navarre asked in a voice that dialed down the anger and ruthlessness as well. More like a conversation between peers.

"That's right," Vinogradov nodded. "We have three trucks. The ride will take about ten minutes."

Stacia watched, but Navarre gave away nothing at all. Just a soft scowl, then he pivoted his face across her camera frame to look back.

"Gunbunnies, split three and three," he yelled. "You have escort."

He pivoted back, never breaking character.

Out of the corner of her eye, Stacia watched the six men jog this direction. The punks got a little more nervous, but nobody provoked Hadiiye, which was good.

Stacia would throw herself to the hot sand and try to burrow to where it got cooler if violence broke out. Anything to be out of the line of fire.

"So let's do this thing," Navarre announced.

Stacia waited a beat as folks started to move, then popped up.

"And CUT!" she yelled. "Good job, people. Nicely done.

This footage will look amazing later."

Heads turned to her like some terrible monster that had emerged from the sands.

Good, she'd been so still most of them had forgotten about her, even that quickly. Of course, Hadiiye and Navarre had helped.

And Aritza/Navarre had warned her that she needed to run her own con.

Distractions.

She walked over the to Witch Doctor.

"When this is done, are you two going to want me to keep your faces and voices visible, or obfuscate everything for the documentary?"

More confusion. Stacia had the sense of quiet chuckles from Navarre, but didn't dare break character herself to check.

"A documentary?" Orlov asked. Like he'd forgotten in the last three minutes.

"That's right," she said. "The deadly and dangerous Navarre. I presume your boss wants to be equally famous and immortalized."

Sounded like pure hokum, a word she'd picked up from Doctor Aritza. Most criminals wanted anonymity in which to hide. At the same time, she was playing to their egos. Their vanity.

Plus, Stacia had gotten more than one subtle suggestion that none of the bad guys might survive whatever *Excalibur*'s crew had planned.

She'd shiver, but it was too hot for that.

Orlov had paused. He shook his head now and tried to regain his stature. Failed, but only barely.

She'd knocked him down a notch.

"We shall see," he said.

Came out weakly. Indecisive, which was the last thing you wanted around predators like this.

Was that Navarre's game? Show them up?

She had no idea, but Suvi was there to protect her if things got rough. Along with everyone else.

"Let's mount up," the bulldog called, looking around.

Stacia nodded when the probe came nerby.

Time to set up the next scene.

Whatever the hell that was.

PART 6

Javier had ended up in the middle truck. Hadiiye, Sascha, and Hajna were riding with him, Mila Vinogradov, the Witch Doctor weirdo, and a handful of local muscle. Throw in Afia, Bethany, and Stacia, and it might look to an outsider like he'd brought a harem with him.

Javier might rupture something laughing at the fool who made that mistake. Granted, he'd slept with three of them, but only three.

And they were all dangerous.

And you could count Suvi and make it seven, if you wanted to list all the women protecting his ass today. She was here, hovering in a high corner of the rear cargo area and presumably filming everything. She had enough memory space in that probe of hers to shoot continuously for about a year without needing to edit the boring parts out.

Nobody needed to know that, though.

Javier was in the middle of the rear row. The interior had a bench for five facing forward, and another facing rear. Couple of punks riding up front with the driver. Couple more stuffed in back with Suvi, because Javier had brought more folks in the main truck than Vinogradov had expected.

Nobody had an assassination planned. At least not yet.

Maybe later.

He was happy betting his life that Hadiiye was better. Especially with the backup she had.

However gorgeous all of them were.

Javier smiled, grinning at the universe.

Vinogradov was directly across from him. She had a hard scowl. Not an unattractive woman, but she didn't seem to care one way or the other, and that conveyed itself as a casual disdain for everyone that moved her into a separate category.

Orlov was the odd bird here. Witch Doctor?

Javier had some level of education. Possibly even erudition, though he'd deny it if pressed.

Witch Doctor suggested a shaman, historically. Bad translation, maybe.

Nobody had ever produced evidence of any sort of paranormal powers, in millennia of trying, so any magic the man claimed to have was crap and prestidigitation. Mind games.

Fellow had a smile like that was his game.

Javier focused his grin on the tall, skinny dork and watched calculations ramp up.

"Tell me about your boss," he commanded in a polite enough voice. Inviting the man to put on a dog and pony show in front of everyone.

Mostly to see where the fool took an open-ended thing like that.

Stacia was filming. She'd been the one to arrange herself on that side, so she was facing Navarre and Suvi was filming Orlov.

And ready to shoot the dumbass if he got stupid.

Javier hated living this sort of existence. The need to expect double-crosses and instant, deadly mayhem. He knew he'd burn out in a hurry if he had to live it for real. Wearing it like a costume for a few weeks was something he could live with.

Probably.

"Zhenya Kovalev leads the pirate horde," Orlov said grandly.

Javier could tell he wanted to gesture as well, but the truck was too confined and he'd end up elbowing somebody in the face if he did that.

Javier nodded to keep the man talking. Suvi had all this footage on tape, and it might even be admissible in a court of law later.

Or at least the court of public opinion.

"*Syntha*'s not a place I care about all that much," Navarre growled back, deeply into anger and superiority. "My gig will be *Valadris*. Far as I can tell, you folks don't ever raid that place, so we shouldn't come into conflict. This, all of this, is mostly a courtesy call on my part so we don't have misunderstandings later."

"You intend to conquer *Valadris*?" Vinogradov asked sharply.

"Hardly," Navarre scoffed. "Folks there are so bent they have to screw their pants on in the morning. No, I'll carve out my space from the underworld of *Valadris* and it will be fine."

At this moment, a perfectly honest player would nod sagely.

Javier figured Stacia was the only perfectly honest person in the truck. Maybe Bethany, too, but she'd talked herself into becoming a pirate herself, so maybe not.

Instead, Vinogradov and Orlov shared a quick glance that spoke volumes to a poker player like him. And the various women around him that he played poker with for large sums. Afia was almost as good a card sharp as Hajna or Sascha, who were, in turn, almost as good as him.

Talk about telegraphing. He just hoped that Suvi and Stacia had gotten that look on film cleanly.

Confession was good for the soul.

"What will you do on *Valadris*?" Vinogradov pressed.

Javier allowed Navarre a scornful laugh.

"I got a warship, pal," he grinned. "Big enough to take anything but major vessels from major players. Nobody around here has anything heavy enough to stop me doing whatever I want, kinda like nobody can stop your plague of locusts from descending on some settlement and stripping it bare."

He watched the calculations in their eyes. Tonnage of killing power against excess of barrels shooting.

Suvi had said that she could probably win, if she got them to come at her in small numbers, like the lesser minions in a chop-socky movie, each waiting their turn to attack the hero.

Smart pirates would all come at her at once.

That was the scenario he needed to eliminate.

Somehow.

"But like I said," Javier continued, "you folks generally operate way over here, so I doubt we'll run into each other all that often."

"Oh, we frequently travel to *Valadris*," Orlov spoke up, not quite challenging, but not willing to be slotted into such a junior varsity position without a least a little fuss.

"Oh?" Javier asked, sounding intrigued and opening his eyes enough to look it as well.

"What he's saying is that we deal with fences on *Valadris* for loot we take from other worlds," Vinogradov interjected sourly. "We do not operate in that vicinity for exactly that reason. However, there are chances we might see each other again after this."

Javier noted the way her eyes didn't seem nearly so malevolent. He wondered if a woman who had a high-ranking position with a group of pirates might need to escape the confines occasionally. Lots of these worlds were chauvinistic cesspools of macho and testosterone, so she might not be able to let her guard down around anybody without looking weak.

She did not look weak. And had a position high in the hierarchy around here, so she had to be remarkably competent. And smart. And dangerous.

Javier's kind of woman, at the end of most days, but anything he did with her would be strictly business. Regardless of how much they might both enjoy it.

"That sounds exceptional," Navarre replied, nodding to the woman like they'd just made a reservation for an assignation sometime in the not-too-distant future.

Whatever it took to eliminate these folks so that worlds like *Byormi* could get on with turning into real places.

You could not con an honest man. Or woman. They wouldn't be consumed by the greed of an inside trick for getting rich. Pirates, at the end of the day, were bullies who took things from people because they could.

Right up until the moment someone made them stop.

Asking politely never worked. You had to punch somebody like that in the mouth. Then maybe knock them down and kick them a few times.

Then get mean.

Still, if seducing this woman opened a schism in the larger organization, that might be a cheaper way to slip a knife home.

He filed it for future reference.

"And you, Captain Navarre?" Orlov spoke up finally. "What do you have planned in this sector?"

"Mostly establishing *Valadris* as a safe harbor," he replied. "Like you, but also a base of operations for longer voyages outward to prey on some of the weaker places around here. Mostly commercial shipping, rather than planetary raids, as I've got the firepower to take big ships and don't need a crew large enough to hit dirtside."

Again, nods, when honest folks would be disgusted or horrified at such behavior.

Honest folks.

Few and far between.

What he had were two packs of killers delicately sniffing at each other. Or so those fools were being led to believe.

You couldn't con an honest man.

"Approaching the palace now," the driver announced from the front seat.

Javier had been watching over Orlov's shoulder as the building got larger out the front window.

Dark stone edifice emerging from the side of a hill. Maybe a volcanic plug or tor of some sort. Like they'd hollowed inward and used all those stones to build out.

Not ugly, but Javier had never been into brutalism as architecture, and he supposed that with a world this hot, you needed a lot of stone overhead to act as a heat sink.

Still, the garage door that opened looked an awful lot like the mouth of a waking dragon.

KOVALEV'S PALACE

PART 1

Bethany found herself in a strange place mentally as the truck came to rest and landed on smooth stone. She was part of Javier's crew, but had been more than a little intimate with Stacia on the flight here, after a conversation in the forward bar had gotten a bit more intense and interesting than she'd expected.

She supposed that she bridged the various worlds, as she was still the newest crew member among Javier's inner circle. The one who had accompanied Afia down to *Valadris* because she was the expert on researching things, once you got out of bars.

Stacia was the outsider, here to get the footage she would need to go home and shake the foundations of Valadrian society. Zakhar had been concerned that Bethany might want to stay and help Stacia with that. Or that Stacia might decide she wanted to travel on with them.

Neither, but that had involved a few conversations in bed where they both came to understand that there was a hard deadline on what they could have.

Odd, but Bethany was getting used to doors closing irrevocably behind her. So far, new ones had opened in the nick of time, and she hadn't ended up as a waitress in a dive where the train tracks came to an end.

That was still possible.

Here, she was putting her training to use. Architecture, and people. The former, because she enjoyed buildings. The latter, because she'd spent a lot of time as a junior officer in a navy shrinking and getting pissy about it.

The pirates around them were mostly young. Three to one male or worse, but she supposed that the adrenaline rush of combat flying drew them. And the freedom from rules and laws, as long as you obeyed Kovalev's word. Or her senior people.

Bethany found herself in the middle of the group as they walked deeper into the building. Behind Navarre and Hadiiye and the two locals. Next to Afia for the most part, with Stacia ranging out ahead with several local goons, ostensibly shooting dramatic footage.

Suvi was probably mapping the place with ultrasonics to the millimeter, in case her other self needed to blow it up at some point. Bethany had seen the specs for the probe.

And nobody was paying much attention to her as they went, which was fine. They encountered a few folks in long corridors that were cooler than the outside, growing more chilled with every meter. Damp as well, but they were inside the mountain now. Sloping slightly down.

Presumably, headed to Kovalev's throne room.

So Bethany watched Orlov and Vinogradov. Studied their walks as a way of looking in their minds.

Too many years of angry Captains and Admirals stomping into her library looking for books that existed only in their imaginations. Survivors developed a sense for the way those people moved.

Both were uncertain. Slightly discombobulated, but not badly.

Neither knew how to deal with Navarre, but that wasn't an uncommon thing.

He only really existed in Javier's mind, after all.

Locals fell into three groups, near as she could tell. Gunbunny wannabes, or at least armed punks.

Second were the pilots. They had a wildness to them. In the way they walked. Or dressed. Or even just stood around watching her pass.

Importance, because they were the ones that flew raider vessels to other worlds and stole things at gunpoint.

Bethany kept her face neutral when looking at them. Not an inviting smile, because she knew what pilots were like. Not a challenging scowl, either.

Finally, and far less visible, were the support staff. Folks who maintained the household. Cooks. Maids. Butlers. Helpers.

She wondered how many of them had come here voluntarily, and how many had been taken in raids.

The women seemed to be pretty, but not acting like it. Like they'd been prettier once, and had lost hope today. Or become slaves of pirates, and knew they existed to serve.

They reminded Bethany why she was helping Javier do this.

Hurting people like Kovalev meant that nameless peons didn't have to be treated like that. They could be free.

What did it say about the state of the galaxy that a ruthless killer like Navarre was necessary to make that happen?

Bethany kept her commentary inside, off her face and out of her eyes. They were approaching a big pair of double doors. Five meters tall and probably three and a half wide.

An architectural statement that made a political one. Presumably the throne room of the Queen of the Pirates herself.

Bethany found herself wondering what kind of a woman Zhenya Kovalev was.

PART 2

Javier followed Stacia into the big room. Orlov and Vinogradov had been largely silent once they got into the building, clamming up so they could pass him and his people off to their boss.

Everyone was armed, which was rude on his part, but he also wasn't here hat in hand asking politely.

Not that they would have listened.

No, he was here in his guise as Apocalyptic Warlord, laying down a new set of rules for other folks to obey.

Or something like that.

The place did not fill him with joy. Too dark, when lighting equipment was cheap. Conscious decision on the part of set designers or somebody who had never emerged from their teenage goth phase.

Fortunately, all photographic evidence of a fourteen-year-old Javier Aritza had been destroyed long since.

No plants in the hallways. No art on the walls, beyond graffiti. Not even stone carvings to break up the monotony of the dark gray slabs around him. Might have been okay if they'd had some sort of sparkling granite with pretty patterns or colors, but this was a dull volcanic rock with no character.

Hopefully not an indication of expectations for the people in charge.

A few folks he saw in the hallways also didn't fill him with joy. Mostly dressed in varieties of beige that would be useful out in the sun and heat. Hardly any colorfulness there either.

He was Navarre in maroon. Hadiiye was in a lavender tunic that went well with her electric purple boots, chest focused with glossy black leather straps and that silver ring between her breasts.

Peacock and peahen, while the rest of you were sparrows.

He scowled and walked.

Through the big doors, Hadiiye held up a hand and silently told the eight killers to array themselves on the walls behind her. Out of the way, but available in an ambush.

She led Javier to the center of a big open space, with a raised stage on the far end and groups of locals on either sides of the room. Again, beige costuming, with a few hints of color mostly concealed underneath.

He caught all that at a glance in Hadiiye's wake, then concentrated on the stage.

Orlov and Vinogradov went up a set of stairs to one side. Rise was about a meter and a quarter. More than he or most folks could jump in a single stride, but not Hadiiye. He wondered if anybody on that side realized that.

Navarre came to rest and studied the woman on her throne. Queen of the Pirates, and all that squamph.

Zhenya Kovalev looked about the same age as Mila Vinogradov. Maybe a couple of years younger. Or softer years. But Vinogradov was broad and bulky. Muscles like a guy, without a gram of fat on her that he'd seen.

Kovalev reminded him of 'Mina. Helped that both were strawberry blondes. 'Mina's hair had been long, the last time he'd seen her, while Kovalev's was almost as short as Djamila's. Not as fauxhawk on top, though.

Physically, a little heavier than Javier liked them, too. 'Mina had been asleep for nearly five centuries, so she'd had an excuse, and gotten back into shape pretty quickly.

Kovalev felt tall. A little squishy, mostly in the large chest and generous hips split by a nice waist, all that evident even contained in pale blue pants and a baggy, white, linen shirt that buttoned up the front and seemed to gap in inviting ways. Buttons straining, as it were.

Freckles, too. Cute ones, at least from what he could see down here. Someone had done an adequate lighting job on the stage. First time he could say that in this place.

Navarre would study Kovalev as competition, then devour her visually as a beautiful woman, so Javier did the same.

Helped offset things, though, when he had women just as beautiful around him. All of them were sharp enough— probably deadly enough—to replace the woman up on that stage if they got that notion in their heads.

He held the tableaux for a little longer than normal, mostly to give everyone time to get to their marks, and for Stacia to arrange her cameras.

He'd been half expecting somebody over there to object to him bringing a documentarian with him. Fools hadn't, but he supposed that they were expecting honor among thieves or something equally stupid from him.

Lady, if you only knew.

Finally, the pause had stretched long enough. Orlov had whispered several things in the woman's ear while they waited and Stacia filmed it all for use in a court later.

"I'm Captain Navarre," he said in a conversational voice, rather than a challenge. "Folks on *Valadris* suggested that you might be the most dangerous pirate in the region, at least until recently, and that I should meet with you and come to certain understandings about the future."

He watched. Orlov said a few more things. Vinogradov came around the other side and offered her two drachmasl worth as well.

"Are you a threat, Navarre?" she asked.

"Not to you," he replied, leering at her beauty to give some level of lie to the words. "But to all the other fools out there..."

"You have heard of the Horde?" she continued.

"Locusts," he nodded. "Land on a village somewhere and strip it bare in hours. Not my gig. Not my competition. I'm going after whales instead."

Offered that way, in that tone, one might choose to take offense, since he was possibly suggesting that she wasn't good enough, dangerous enough, to go after the kinds of big game he hunted.

Navarre was, after all, a thing many folks feared. Especially as more of them heard about *Meehu* or *Nidavellir*.

Stone killer.

A man might take those words as a challenge. Wiring and chemistry thing, where they often had to whip their dicks out and measure them, however metaphorically.

Hopefully, she didn't think that way.

Of course, if she did, he could certainly find a meat grinder somewhere to lead her and her horde of maniacs into.

Javier waited.

Her eyes got shrewd. Deadly, even. Around him, he heard whispers and murmurs from the folks down here on ground level.

The crazy ones who might have to wave their dicks around to prove something.

He'd known enough pilots in his time. Del was merely forty or more years older than most of them. Same level of crazy.

"Who are you here to kill, Navarre?" she asked, showing him that she'd done her homework, at least.

Captain Navarre was as much a thief and assassin as a killer. Folks forgot about *Shangdu* occasionally, since it hadn't made the news with the same fervor.

"Don't have any names as yet," he fired back, eyes locked with the woman and ignoring the stirs around him.

He had Hadiiye and her killers covering his back. He could focus on Kovalev.

Her hold on the mob didn't feel as solid as it had a few moments ago.

Whatever it took to break them all.

"Got anybody you need killed?" he asked a moment later in a tone just enough short of sneering condescension that she could ignore it if she chose.

Woman's eyes flared a bit at that. Like maybe he was just another sexist pig suggesting that she wasn't tough enough to handle her own battles.

Five card stud, lady. Jacks or better to open.

Around him, the locals started getting a little more rowdy. Not much. Not yet.

Still, it was a wedge. Lots of dangerous yahoos who appeared to be held in place by her brains and personality. Beauty was frosting on top.

Kovalev hadn't parachuted into the gig and been anointed. Rumors suggested a former fighter pilot from somewhere who was Del's peer at crazy flying. And lethality. Worked her way up then took over.

But it was always a young person's game.

Javier had fought against growing old as hard as the next guy, but he'd be forty-four, next birthday. Time to grow up and act like management, as Zakhar liked to remind him occasionally.

"Why are you here, Navarre?" she snapped.

"I'm here to meet the only person in the sector dangerous enough to matter, Kovalev," he replied, offering a concession that wasn't wrapped up in sexual politics.

"Rather deal with you than fight you. Cops win if we did that."

She nodded. Hot-headed, but not as desperately offended as most of his probable answers would have gotten her.

Gotta boil this frog slow, after all. If he wanted out of his room alive. Off the planet alive.

He was mostly pushing to see where the fault lines were. Because if he could get her or Vinogradov over into a realm of man and woman, instead of enemy pirates, he had a lot of ways to get to them.

Helped, when he had experts advising him on the best ways to understand any given woman.

Kovalev's chin came up. Not much. Challenging, nonetheless.

Her eyes looked blue, but that might be the lighting. Or his warm memories of 'Mina.

"So let's talk," she said, tone challenging his manhood in all the ways a smart woman could.

That made her all the more dangerous.

Javier smiled. Or rather, Navarre would have, and he saw no reason to forbid it.

Instead, he took a long, penetrating look around, rotating in place and noting the mobs on both sides. Maybe forty or fifty each directly, though he'd really ignored them previously. Pilots and base staff. A few who looked like merchants here to buy or sell stuff. Fences or mouthpieces. Maybe an accountant or three.

"You and two, me and two?" he asked, nodding towards Afia and Bethany. "Plus one guerrilla filmmaker who's going to make me over into a statesman by the time she's done?"

That caught everyone off guard. He was volunteering to not have his killers around, and instead bring only his fixers? Plus Stacia, who upset all calculations because she didn't fit into any of them.

Which might be exactly why he'd sought her out and brought her along.

Navarre smiled.

Poker was a game of personality, not mathematics. Unlike chess or go. You could win with a weak hand, or lose with a strong one.

The play, and the players, mattered.

"Alright," she nodded, knowing that his words contained a trap, but unable to see it.

Because she wasn't dreaming *nearly* big enough.

Occupational hazard with pirates. All the drama of junior high, with deadly encounters thrown in. If they'd wanted to grow up and act like adults, they wouldn't have ended up here.

Kovalev rose. Tall, long, lean, and gorgeous.

Shame.

She gestured to a couple of goons handy, then at Hadiiye, having understood what that woman's job was.

"Orlov, get Navarre's other folks settled in rooms," she ordered. "Then join us."

Navarre stood still in the middle of the chamber as Orlov waved the locals out. Hadiiye, Afia, and Bethany stayed put. Stacia filmed things.

Pretty quickly, it was them, plus Kovalev, Vinogradov, and a couple of her own bodyguards. Professional-enough looking, but not in Hadiiye's league, to say nothing of Djamila's.

"This way, Captain Navarre," Kovalev nodded crisply. "Let's get a little more comfortable, then we can talk."

He nodded back.

Now was when it would start to get dangerous. Everything to this point had been merely foreplay.

As it were.

PART 3

Stacia would have even bought it all if she hadn't just spent a week with Doctor Aritza on the ship, listening to him and his people game these things out.

Navarre-the-killer, here to do a rogue's deal with Kovalev. When they had really been trying to find the ways to break those people, and do it in such a way that she could then return to *Valadris* and cauterize the other end of that criminal connection.

A couple of the people in the audience chamber had been dressed in the latest fashions back from home, so she'd made sure to get clean images of their faces for later.

Evidence, as Aritza had proclaimed. Damning evidence, considering the rest of the footage.

Kovalev led them through a door at the back of the stage to what felt like an isolated section of the palace. Away from the pilots and staff. Safe for Kovalev.

Because she was shooting everything, Stacia made sure to stay close to Kovalev's people, mostly watching backwards and getting shots of Navarre and his crew. Supposedly. Acting innocent, because she was unarmed and only a threat if they woke up and realized where all this was leading.

But Aritza had claimed that he could bamboozle the best of them.

Nicer corridors back here. Lots of light. Walls painted in brighter colors than the stone.

Vinogradov and that Witch Doctor weirdo led everyone to a side chamber that felt like a dining hall. Complete with a wooden hutch that had plates and goblets behind glass. Nice ones, too. Expensive stuff.

Stacia assumed that it had caught somebody's eye when some rich rancher got killed and her home stripped by pirates, but she kept her opinions to herself.

Aritza was a tool she was hoping to use as much as he was using her. Everyone came out ahead with these people gone.

Forever.

Kovalev sat at the head of the table. Stacia expected Navarre to sit at the foot, facing her, but he put Afia there and moved around to sit on the far side from the door, about midway down. Leaving only one chair between him and Vinogradov. Was that important?

Bodyguards took up spots on the wall, with Hadiiye behind Navarre.

Stacia studied the social dynamics.

"Probe. Access Command Node," she said aloud. "Move to the corner over Afia's left shoulder and begin filming."

That put Suvi and her gun where she could see and hit anything, as well as putting the best sensors and cameras at an angle that would catch both Kovalev and Navarre in frame while talking.

She moved around and hip-checked a bodyguard slightly out of her way, so that she was over the pirate woman's right shoulder. Not far from the door, but able to see Afia's face mostly square, and Bethany's directly.

Kovalev gestured at the situation. At Stacia.

"What is this, Navarre?" she asked, more confused than disgruntled.

"Making a documentary about the life of piracy," Navarre laughed in an ugly voice. "Recruiting tool for later, so folks see the bright, exciting bits, rather than the tedium of day-to-day operations. Also, to convince folks around here that I'm a modern day Robin Hood, here to rob only from the rich while providing them exciting daydreams and maybe sticking it to people they don't like, either."

"Really?" the woman asked dryly.

"Nobody likes oligarchs," Navarre said, still mirthful. "Too much jealousy. Right now, you get the wish fulfillment aspect of watching them and their money, but if folks like me start hitting those people and stealing their solid iridium toilets, that also plays well. That's why I go after big targets and not random people."

Stacia felt the man next to her bristle at Navarre's words, but he remained silent.

Again, she'd have fallen for all this without knowing Aritza's secret. And she could see what an expert he was on human nature, to be able to say all these things without pushing.

Not *insulting*, unless they *chose* to be insulted. At which point, it was their problem, not his.

Djamila Sykora had taken Stacia to watch in the stands when the tall woman ran a combat obstacle course, mostly to give her an understanding of how dangerous that Amazonian killer was.

Nobody in this room was fast enough to stop the Dragoon killing all of Kovalev's people. And the pirate herself.

"And who do you plan to attack?" Kovalev asked next.

"My targets are out a ways," he nodded. "Corewards some, and primarily in the direction of Earth. Older colonies. Some of the oldest, in fact, if you go far enough. Lots of money over there, but generally no great appetite to chase me this far. In fact, lots of them are like *Valadris*. Independent worlds rather than parts of more powerful stellar nations. As long as the bounties don't get too high, they won't band together and bring enough of a fleet to be a problem."

"Like the *Concord*?" Orlov asked in a knowing, almost sneering voice.

Stacia was almost exactly behind the Witch Doctor, so she hoped that Suvi had him in focus.

"The *Concord* is officially pissed at me for *Nidavellir*," Navarre-the-killer shrugged, turning serious now. "However, private channels let me know that they appreciated me destroying those people. It was in my best interests to be elsewhere for a while, though."

"Killing other pirates?" Vinogradov asked in a hard voice.

"They started it, lady," Navarre scowled. "Twice, as a matter of fact. I got hired to hit a target aboard *Shangdu*. Folks *assumed* a mass casualty incident after what I did to that asshole at *Meehu*. *Expected* it, even, without paying me for such an outcome. Got pissy when I executed the letter of the contract without killing anyone at all. Nothing worse than a single guard stunned unconscious as I made my escape. As a result, they sent warships after me. Pissed me off, so I put paid to them." He paused for effect. "All of them."

Stacia felt the temperature of the room plummet at his words. At the number of people Navarre was acknowledged to have killed, when he had, in fact, killed none of them. Teague did *Meehu*, according to eyewitnesses Stacia had interviewed. Sokolov and Suvi did *Nidavellir*.

Everyone forgot Navarre's team. He'd told her that, but she hadn't understood at the time.

Not until this moment.

Navarre didn't take the credit out of an overabundance of ego, but to let everyone else vanish into his shadow.

Because Captain Eutropio Navarre didn't exist.

He was a fairy tale conjured to frighten children and criminals.

Shit.

He smiled at her now, like he could read her mind. Stacia let her face fall perfectly neutral before anybody else saw. Hopefully.

"So I'm supposed to believe you?" Kovalev asked. "Just like that?"

"You do whatever you think best, Kovalev," he countered. "Makes me no difference at all. None. I'm here because I'd rather come to a consensus that doesn't involve me having to destroy you and your people out of hand because you got in my way later."

The matter of fact way he said that took Stacia's breath away. Worse, because she didn't think he was bluffing. The only reason he hadn't killed the three leaders in the room was that it wouldn't change anything. Others would rise up and take their places, just as Kovalev had done. Possibly by sunset.

Piracy was a lifestyle, and Kovalev hadn't formed this gang. Nobody was sure who had, in fact. Zhenya Kovalev was merely the person currently in charge, having killed or forced out her predecessor.

Interestingly, Afia Burakgazi shook things up now.

"So what do the pirates of *Syntha* need to make them comfortable with the fact that we're also going to be operating in this region?" the tiny woman asked.

And did so in a methodical, professional voice that reminded everyone listening that she could speak for Navarre, even when he was at the table.

Kovalev took a clue and nodded to her Witch Doctor.

Bosses, handing off the hard work of negotiating a deal. And everything on film for later.

"There are a set of about twenty worlds," Orlov said. "A rough sphere, more or less centered on *Syntha* itself."

"Your current victims," Afia nodded.

Orlov bristled, then got over himself as Stacia watched.

"Exactly," he said. "Perhaps another ten that we might wish to hit. Or perhaps even add to our rotation at some point, because they're growing big enough, rich enough, to be worth the effort."

"I'll need a list," Afia replied. "But as he said, we're not looking at the penny ante stuff around here. Our targets are well beyond that. And spaceborn, rather than targets on a planetary surface. What about *Valadris*?"

"What about it?" Vinogradov asked, breaking her silence.

"We're going to be operating out of there, however quietly," Afia answered. "They anyone you ever bother? Or have on a future list?"

"Hell, no," the bulldog laughed. "Most of our commercial and industrial goods are at least sourced out of *Valadris* at present. We've got fingers and connections in a variety of places and industries, to the point we're largely untouchable."

Stacia wanted to growl. Wanted to slap someone.

At the same time, she'd never been able to prove anything in her research. Never. Anywhere. Witnesses either clammed up or simply disappeared, sometimes turning up dead, face down in the water.

And now a bunch of juvenile delinquents were casually discussing details in front of her. And Suvi.

"The governor one of yours?" Bethany asked, suddenly leaning forward and bringing her amazing mind to bear on the conversation. "Our concern had been whether or not we needed to bring down the entire government, or at least the current administration, in order to have peace while we operated."

"Not him, but a few folks in his inner circle," Vinogradov replied. "The man himself is a pretty moron. Great on camera. About as dumb as a mud fence post most of the time. He's largely a front for a number of different criminal organizations. Or groups that would be criminals, but they've successfully twisted the laws around in such a way that most of what they do is technically legal."

"Really?" Navarre asked. "I might want to ask someone a bit more about that. Makes my life so much easier if I only have to buy off a few folks and not engage in certain activities while hanging out at *Valadris*. All the shit I intend to pull will be elsewhere, so none of the locals have to worry. In fact, if you want to get me some names to contact when I get home, I'll happily cut you in on a finder's fee, because you'll already be saving me a lot of bribes and hassle before I ever set foot on *Valadris* again."

Stacia wanted to scream. Tilt her head back and let half a dozen years' worth of rage out in a sound that might shatter glass and eardrums.

And lives.

Instead, she had to remain perfectly still. Perfectly quiet. Utterly at peace as a group of criminals discussed subversion and revolution right in front of her.

She knew that Aritza was doing it on purpose, but she never could have imagined that it would actually work.

Then she caught a profile of Mila Vinogradov with a glance. Turned her own head while keeping the camera still, so she could watch the Second-in-Command.

Kovalev was dominant. Dominating. She had the personality, as well as the looks.

Vinogradov had the brains. Had the growl that made her a good leader.

She didn't have that beauty that caused men to pant. Stacia knew she was cute, but not stunning. Short and petite, when most men wanted long and buxom. Like Kovalev. Hips and chest and a perfect nose.

Stacia wondered how open-minded the top woman might be, but decided that Navarre was probably setting himself up to seduce her. To get inside her mind as a way of getting inside her organization.

Setting them up for the fall.

But for a moment, Stacia saw the rage in Vinogradov's eyes. Never pretty enough, so she'd had to be tougher than all the men. Meaner.

Stacia's mother had talked about such women, and the butch, bitch role that a male-dominated society would often thrust upon them. Usually Stacia learned those things as part of a lesson on deportment. Fashion. Makeup. Carriage.

Something to make men notice you. Ogle you. Lust after you.

Underestimate you, because that had been Mother's game. Let the men think they were in charge, while twisting their minds with her whispers, until they did what she wanted, never realizing that it wasn't their own idea.

Stacia had never seen a man—even one like Navarre—understand that. Let alone execute it.

While she watched, Orlov turned to Kovalev. The bitch in charge nodded, and Stacia could see a list of names with pirate connections suddenly taking shape in the man's head, where it would be handed over to Navarre-the-killer with nothing more than a promise of future bribes.

Because money under the table was how society worked more often than not. Even *Valadris*.

Maybe especially *Valadris*, since she was getting her mind expanded about how corrupt outsiders saw her homeworld.

"Finder's fee?" Vinogradov asked leadingly.

Her eyes had held a promise of contained rage. The knowledge that she had to handle all the work while Kovalev got the credit.

"That, and your thirty worlds you want marked off limits," Afia replied. "Won't promise anything without seeing the list, but if they are all local to you, I doubt any of them are on our scanners. As Navarre said, we're going long-sailing for big whales in the deep water. Our need is *Valadris* remaining neutral to us, and not having to constantly watch our backs about other pirates. As he notes, there's been some bad blood with other fools, and he generally has a low trust. Still, nothing personal, so nothing you have to worry about."

Stacia wondered how many of the people who had traveled here on *Excalibur* could teach college or graduate level courses, were someone to open a university of criminal behavior. These were not skills one just picked up on the streets. They had to have come from hard work and harder lives.

Even Bethany admitted to being something of a babe in the woods, compared to Aritza or Sokolov.

And then there was Stacia McNulty.

"How long are you staying on the ground?" Kovalev asked.

All heads turned to Navarre.

"Depends on you," he replied with a half-shrug that carried no emotional weight at all. "We could remain exactly long enough to get data from your Witch Doctor then depart. Or stay overnight if you wanted to throw a banquet. Not looking to hang around long enough to join you on some raid, unless you were planning to take off in the morning. Then I might be open to *negotiating*."

The way he stressed that last word made Stacia want to take a long shower with a lot of soap and a brush to get the ickiness off her skin. Him and Kovalev fucking as a way of sealing a deal, like a pair of wild animals in spring, coming together long enough to mate before heading back to their own hunting grounds.

And about as much emotion as buying a bottle of tea at the corner shop.

She wondered if the pirates really were that primitive and brutal.

At the same time, Mother's lessons on social power

bubbled up. Neither Kovalev nor probably Vinogradov could have any sort of physical relationship with any one of their underling pirates, lest that one get a swelled head at their own importance.

Maybe she had a harem, like Navarre seemed to be dangling in front of everyone with all the women who accompanied him?

No men beyond the six killers outside and Mr. Smith piloting.

Still, ick.

"Negotiating?" Kovalev asked in that long, drawled way that just oozed sex and carnality all over things.

Yet another type of social combat?

Hopefully, nobody would demand her skills as a pornographer tonight.

There were limits, even if she had only now discovered one of them.

"You know," Navarre purred at the woman. "You scratch my back and I'll scratch yours?"

"We'll see," Kovalev said. "For now, let's banquet and toast new deals and new beginnings. Then maybe we can discuss *other things*."

Stacia waited a long beat, but things seemed to have hit the perfect emotional crescendo. Or something. She still wanted a shower.

"And, **CUT!**"

PART 4

Javier was in a suite that Kovalev had assigned him. Big central chamber for hosting and talking. Half a dozen sleeping chambers, two of which had en-suite bathrooms to go with a third by the front door.

Enough space to contain all his folks comfortably, with Del having flown back up to *Excalibur* for now.

Sascha and Hajna had taken out a pair of hand scanners Javier had originally designed and were giving the place a good going-over. Suvi had better tools, but he wanted that to be a surprise, assuming that there were bugs and cameras in here watching and listening.

Not that he planned to break character in any way. Still, he'd like to relax a little.

Hadiiye stood in such a location that she covered the best sight lines for killing things, but Djamila would have done that anyway. Iqbal and his crew were spread out and alert, already working into rotations for pairs to stay awake all night on guard duty.

Stacia looked like she's swallowed a live goldfish, but he

already knew that she was far too innocent for the life she'd chosen.

Part of the reason he'd picked her out, at the end of the day. The other reporters—the older ones—tended to start cutting corners. Maybe making deals with some of the folks they were supposedly investigating. Maybe ignoring friends that gave them evidence and clues to destroy enemies.

Yeah, he knew how that cutthroat business worked.

Afia and Bethany sat side by side on the couch, more or less facing him. He could tell that Stacia wanted to sit, but she had a role to play, so she was still filming, hand camera on him while Suvi just happened to be in a place where she could cover things as well.

"Captain Navarre, why would you simply accept a list of worlds not to hit?" Stacia asked in her interviewing voice.

Playing a role.

"We aren't in competition with Kovalev's people," he replied with a nod that would look good in her later footage, even blurred out some. "They come out of jump low, dive quickly into an atmosphere, and hit the ground at some target before most folks can react."

"Wouldn't a planetary militia be able to stop them?" she asked earnestly.

Gods, he couldn't ever remember being that innocent.

"Like a volunteer fire department, McNulty," he growled, staying in character himself. "The alert goes out, and folks gather up to do something. But fires don't shoot back. Aren't trying to kill you. If you were constantly facing pirates, you'd be better off hiring killers. Guns are tools, but killing someone is a skill. A way of thinking that most people aren't prepared to deal with. The pirates have no qualms about shooting someone, so they'll generally win."

"So a militia…?"

"Might work," he shrugged. "If the pirates landed where the locals could gather up and hit them fast. Maybe if you had a good colonel in charge, and a budget for gear better than the pirates. Both expensive propositions. I'm guessing that most worlds on that list are primarily farming. Thin economic margins. Thin population density, spread out over huge swaths of the countryside for ranching or farming. World gets larger, cities start forming. Those population centers need cops, which can also deputize folks and maybe get dangerous. Those thirty worlds are likely all primary economies. Mining, extraction, farming. Maybe a little light industry, but no factories of any note."

"Would they move on to bigger worlds?" Stacia asked.

"Risks go up quickly," he nodded. "Maybe the payoffs are better, but chances are you start suffering significant casualties on any given raid. Farms are easier, because you can overwhelm someone. If you don't plan to kill anyone, landing a few hundred armed yahoos is a good way for a few families to stand around while you steal some of their cattle."

"Only some?" Stacia asked, surprised.

He shook his head.

"Pirates are parasites, in the most technical sense of the word, McNulty," he said, turning back into a Doctor of Botany for a moment. "If they kill the host, they starve, because you won't see big herds of cattle or pigs around here. Those will get slaughtered as quickly as they can and frozen. Maybe there's a mobile slaughterhouse that travels with them. Similarly, if you steal all their tractors and such, the farmers can't make any more food and have to leave. Eventually, the planet stops being viable. It is a delicate balancing act, which is why they have some twenty places they hit in rotation. Maybe every four to eight weeks for the next target, but so many means years might pass. Long enough to recover."

"And your plan to hit freighters?" she asked.

"Whales," he replied. "Big ship where everything is already packed for me. Not all the equipment aboard will be useful, but the mass alone means I can sell it to fences on

Valadris for a tonnage fee, after pulling out the valuable things for individual negotiations. Hell, the hulls alone will be worth a lot of money. That's why getting a list of names from Kovalev will save me so much time. Don't have to bribe little players until I work my way up to the ones that can digest an entire cargo ship. Happy to cut her in on that. I could go hit someone and drag that whale's carcass to *Valadris* and sell it immediately. Win/win."

"What about the crews?" she asked.

Javier felt his face turn hard. And his voice.

"Unless they give me a reason otherwise, they all get home safe," he said simply. "Those are folks doing a job. Just happened to be in the wrong place at the wrong time. No reason they have to pay for the foolishness of their bosses. Only folks I've ever killed in this line of business were pirates, after all. If you have a reputation for being a bloodthirsty maniac, folks will fight you to the death. On the other hand, if I am known for mercy, folks will be more likely to surrender without putting up a stupid fight. I'm also a parasite that way. I happen to have a much clearer understanding of how to be successful at it."

She paused there, face inscrutable as he watched her.

"And CUT!" she said, putting her camera into her pocket a moment later.

Javier nodded. Suvi was still recording, but that was not footage for Stacia, and might be deleted later.

He watched the woman slide around and settle on the couch next to Bethany, with Afia on her other side leaning in like both women were sharing their warmth with Stacia. Might be. Javier didn't know if she liked boys, but most of the crew were fairly nondenominational that way.

Made things work better.

"Now, what?" she asked in a softer voice.

They were still on camera, though, until Sascha or Hajna said otherwise.

"Now, we go have dinner with these fine folks in a few hours," he replied. "Toast and boast and make general fools of ourselves in the interests of socially lubricating a tentative alliance of convenience. They don't have much of anything I want, beyond that list. I doubt I have much they want, other than maybe she proposes we do join them on some raid."

"Would you?" Stacia asked, sounding like idle curiosity if you couldn't see her eyes.

Like he could.

"Maybe," Navarre shrugged. Javier was even more ambivalent. "Our ship doesn't land, so we can't really help them there, unless she decides to hit someplace that has orbital defenses because we could help crush those. Flip side, she might want to load a crew of us onto one of her ships so we can go *a-viking* together."

"A-what?"

"Old Earth term," he smiled. "*A-viking* means something like going raiding. Vikings were terrible warriors from the northern part of Europe, back in the Iron Age. Also incredibly socially advanced at the time, but they get bad PR from historians, most of whom were on the losing end of those pirate raids. For the Vikings, raids were a way to build prestige and wealth. Plus, there were religious war elements, when they were off hitting Christian kingdoms while they were primarily pagans."

"Would you go?" Stacia asked.

Hadiiye stirred exactly enough to turn her head his way with a disapproving scowl, but that was Djamila. The character Hadiiye would have been laughing and charging, most likely.

"Lots of *maybes* and *it depends* in there," he said. "Trust most of those people about as far as I can throw 'em. Isolating me from the ship is also a risk. I could see Del wanting to borrow some sled, though. Hadiiye, did you see any vessels at the landing field that looked big enough to carry a crew of twelve to twenty? Us, plus some of Kovalev's folks?"

"Six," Hadiiye replied simply.

Knowing Djamila, she and Del had hard-scanned them on approach and she could tell anybody who asked everything they wanted to know.

Killers took their craft just as seriously as musicians.

He nodded to both women, as if that covered it.

Javier rose.

"For now, I'm going to take a quick nap," he announced.

Not that he would sleep, but some meditation would be good for dealing with what was likely coming. Probably a long night ahead of him.

PART 5

Djamila understood that Javier didn't want to run this operation with the sort of military precision that she could bring to the table.

Or, as he liked to call it, pretending he had a weak hand, to entice some fool into calling and raising.

Setting them up for the kill later.

Still, she was Hadiiye, and a killer. Plus, two pathfinders and six gunslingers who all met her standards on a quarterly basis.

She brought that eye to the situation. Studied every tactical angle. Every person she encountered.

Always prepared to kill.

That she was the good guys these days was just weird, but nothing much had changed otherwise.

She escorted Navarre through a few hallways to a second grand chamber from the place they'd been before. Dining hall, closer to the exit. Trestle tables in six short rows. Folding metal with plastic tops covered over with cloth from the shapes underneath. No chairs, as everyone sat on benches.

A single row athwart that at the top of the room, where Kovalev and her people would sit facing the rest of the pirates.

Roughly one hundred people in here right now, mostly chatting amongst themselves, pausing as she led Navarre, Afia, and Bethany into the room, with all her people a comm call away from either her or Suvi's probe. Technically, she was following Emman Orlov as he walked with that stupid staff tapping the stone floor every time his right foot landed.

That sound was what caused the silence.

Djamila sized up the room as she kept walking. A few of the folks were armed. Mostly knives, but some pistols. Hopefully, nobody feeling crazy enough to start a gunfight in here. Navarre was armed, and potentially dangerous, if he had a large enough crowd to shoot into.

She would rely on Suvi.

Stacia was already here. Had come early and been interviewing pirates, accompanied by her floating camera. She had her handheld on Javier now, recording all this like a movie.

Perhaps Piet and Suvi would offer to create a soundtrack for her later. They both had large catalogs of available music to work with. Not much of it to Djamila's taste, but exceptional work, to hear others talk about it.

Orlov led Navarre to the head table, then indicated a spot on the wall nearby where Hadiiye could stand and watch. She nodded and worked to turn as invisible as this outfit would allow. Lights overhead probably lit up the silver ring between her breasts in such a way as to draw all attention there.

Wilhelmina's original design to distract.

Vinogradov was there when Navarre sat. She had a quick conversation with Navarre and the two women while Djamila watched, but it seemed mostly idle pleasantries. The crowd quickly ignored them as staff began delivering bread in bowls and pouring drinks. Mostly coffee and tea, so apparently even

Kovalev wasn't arrogant enough to mix alcohol with armed pirates and strangers.

Then the pirate herself entered. Interestingly, she didn't make a scene. Didn't require her people to rise and wait on her. Instead, she walked over and sat down, with Orlov joining her a moment later.

Let the party begin.

PART 6

Afia assumed that it had been done on purpose, putting her next to Kovalev, with the Witch Doctor on her far side and Bethany beyond that. Happened to put Javier on the woman's far side, with the hard First Officer Vinogradov beyond Javier.

Boxed in by women, just how he liked it. But that was Javier. Most men would probably let that sort of thing go to their heads.

She kept an eye sideways in case he needed rescuing from the two babes and listened as Orlov cleared his throat. Sounded like business at this end of the table.

Which was her job.

"What is the state of your logistics?" he asked, glancing back and forth at her and Bethany.

Navarre's accountants, at least in his mind.

Not all that far from the truth, if you squinted just right.

"We loaded full at *Valadris*," Afia replied while Bethany leaned closer to listen. "Solid stockpiles of dry goods for at least ten weeks at current consumption. Frozen roughly the same. Fresh will run out sooner, but we've got hydroponics and aquaponics aboard and both are running efficiently."

The man blinked like she'd booped him on the nose. Probably hadn't been prepared for experts.

There was a reason Zakhar sent her to deal with resupply on every new planet they visited. Bethany was the research babe filling Suvi's mind with new data, then helping her process it down into more sneakiness.

"Captain Kovalev will be proposing a joint raid to Captain Navarre," he said, dropping his voice. "Navarre and part of his crew flying with her, either aboard her flagship, or accompanying."

"You want our ship to remain here?" Afia asked, bristling verbally at the man.

He might be tall. She could still take that stupid stick away from him and beat his ass to death with it, given any reason.

"On the contrary," he countered quickly, backpaddling out of whitewater. "You will join us. The world in question has some defenses. Nothing grand, but having a warship overhead will mean that we can climb out after the attack without worrying about anybody hitting us at that moment when we are most at risk."

"That's up to Navarre," Afia growled. "Sokolov is former *Concord* Navy. And a captain with them. He'll command that aspect of things, assuming Navarre agrees. What's in it for us?"

"A larger share of the treasure taken," Orlov replied.

"We don't need tractors or stolen grain," she laughed harshly. "Unless you're going someplace with an industrial backbone worth stealing, not anything I'd recommend."

She said it in such a way that he would understand that her vote mattered to Navarre. That he had a crew of experts.

Kovalev had two, as near as Afia could tell. Plus a lot of folks on those lower tables probably itching to move up some.

She wondered how many of them were men. Most of the folks at the lower end of the room were male. Maybe three to one sex ratio at a quick eyeball.

"Your assistance means we can do exactly that," Orlov preened at her. Smiling like the cat with the canary in its mouth.

"Where?" Bethany chimed in, dragging the man's head around.

"*Surayya*," he replied.

Afia gave Bethany a questioning look. Got a quick nod back.

"Step up from your usual prey," Bethany offered, confirming Afia's suspicion.

"As noted, your ship means we can tackle a larger foe," Orlov said. "If orbital space is not at risk, we can bring the entire horde with us and make the grandest statement this organization ever has."

That was exactly what Afia was afraid of.

PART 7

Javier smiled and enjoyed himself as Navarre was currently the center of attention of two highly competent, extremely deadly women. If only one of them was a stunning beauty, the other wasn't anybody he'd kick out of bed for eating crackers.

Skin deep, and all that.

Both had ugly souls, but who was he to point fingers?

Navarre wasn't here to romance them, save to set the two up. Pirates who needed to be destroyed before they escaped.

Storm Gauntlet's crew had gotten away with it, after all, but that was because Javier had been in a position where he needed them to destroy somebody even worse.

Lots of somebodies.

And besides, *Storm Gauntlet*'s crew hadn't been nearly as bad as their reputation, once he was aboard as a Centurion.

But Djamila and Bethany both had accurate points when they looked at him and invoked the old samurai mythos, though he preferred the cowboy instead.

Different kind of honor.

Still a cold, deadly son of a bitch.

Sitting immediately next to him, Mila Vinogradov didn't clean up all that bad. He was close enough to smell the breath mint she'd had recently enough to matter. Rough skin. Squarish kind of face that didn't have any prominent features save deadly brown eyes. Reminded him of his second wife that way.

Fryda hadn't been a great beauty, either. Merely convinced that she could get him to clean up his act. One of these days, he'd manage to find her to send an apology letter. He owed her that much.

Nothing more, though, 'cause hopefully she had a better life now than what they'd had together and it would be unacceptably rude for him to show up and upset that.

Still, he could smile at Mila. Flirt with her, which she seemed to appreciate.

Zhenya Kovalev, on his other side, had a lovely perfume on that seemed to embrace him. And a perfect nose, ever so slightly upturned in a way that made her look almost like a pixie. One almost as tall as him.

"How serious are you, Navarre?" Mila asked, drawing him away from his tea and a rye bread that wasn't all that bad for pirate fare.

"Could you narrow that down?" he parried, smiling just enough to make it humorous. "Lots of possibilities in such a question. Which ones did you have in mind?"

And double and triple entendres, because why the hell not? Both women were smart enough to fence with him verbally, which made it all the better.

"Departing on a raid in the morning, if we had one set up," Zhenya said, turning a little less coquettish and a shade more serious.

Although, maybe piracy was an aphrodisiac to the woman. Women.

He'd known weirder folks in his time.

"Depends on who you wanna hit," he shrugged, glancing back and forth at the byplay on either side of him.

Set up, but weren't they all?

Wasn't like Navarre was on the level or anything.

"*Surayya*," Mila offered.

"Don't know the place," he replied.

Suvi would. Probably Zakhar as well. And Bethany. That was the joy of a competent crew. He didn't have to do everything himself. Not like these two women and their Witch Doctor.

"A step up from our usual targets," Zhenya said. "More industrial. More wealth."

"Need a warship in orbit to keep the yahoos from getting obstreperous?" he asked.

"Perhaps," she nodded. "They don't have any significant orbital defenses, but could get a few squadrons in a blocking point, in the hours we'd be on the ground. Nothing that could challenge us, but a ship launching is in a position of weakness until they clear the atmosphere enough to maneuver without tumbling."

He nodded. Del always talked about that. Part of the reason the shuttle had a turret. Might not mean shit against *Excalibur*, but a handful of local snubfighters might be able to wreak a petite form of havoc if they could sit above you at rest, nose down and riding the gyros while they shot.

Kovalev's ships didn't carry shields. Maybe a few of the bigger ones did, but even then more for navigational hazards than combat.

"Sure," he continued. "I can keep overwatch."

"Actually, we wanted to see you in action down on the ground," Mila replied.

As traps went, it wasn't half bad. He could dance around it and refuse, but they'd get pissy. Spread rumors that Navarre was a physical coward, to the point he'd have to do something magnificently stupid again.

221

Another *Shangdu*, maybe.

On the other hand, him on the ground opened up all sorts of possibilities for accidents. Like back in the bad old days with the Dragoon.

That knife cut both ways, as Djamila had always liked to remind him.

"You thinking my shuttle?" he asked. "Can haul a lot of folks to the ground, but it's not jump-equipped."

"Or you could ride aboard my raider," Mila countered. "You brought nine killers with you, plus the blonde with the camera. The other two can remain with your ship. I've got space for a few days if we sleep a little rough and maybe double up. You don't mind that sort of coziness, do you?"

He'd wondered which woman might make the first pass at him. Sounded like Zhenya was going first, and Mila would try her luck on the flight out, then.

Most men's egos would get the best of them right now. Thinking with their dicks, as the ancient saying went.

Fortunately, he'd mostly been cured of that silliness.

Mostly.

He grinned at the woman, figuring that cozy probably meant her bunk. He wondered if it was a standard narrow one where you couldn't roll over with somebody in there. Great way to get lousy sleep.

There was a reason he had an oversized bed in *Excalibur*. And not just for company. A good night's rest was the start of a good day.

"You want my shuttle pilot as well?" Javier asked. "He might be a little put out to miss something like this. You should have heard him laughing on the flight in."

For the tiniest moment, Javier saw a sourness in Mila's eyes. Hardly even a blink, but exactly the sort of tell that bad poker players never overcame.

Told him volumes about the woman.

And possibly of at least one of the double-crosses she had in mind.

"Is he any good?" she asked with hardly enough hesitation to notice.

"Depends," Javier replied. "How good were those five punks that decided to try their luck with him?"

"Amateurs looking to build reputation," she lied.

Another tell, watching her. Someone had sent up some of their better pilots, possibly to kill him and make it look accidental. Just like Djamila in the old days.

If he'd had any doubts about what these two women had planned before, Mila's face put lie to it all.

"Then he's about in the middle, compared to your folks," Javier lied back, watching her. "Been good enough for me, but I'm guessing you have someone better flying you around."

"I pilot myself," Mila said in a hard voice.

"Oh?" he leered at her. "Then maybe you'll have to take me for a ride sometime."

He let his eyes fall, taking in her physicality as a woman, like a dumb punk who thought with his dick.

Back in school, he'd had a buddy once give Javier the single best piece of advice he'd ever ignored until much, much later.

Eventually, Jerry had said, *you have to roll over and talk to her.*

It had only taken Javier twenty years to understand what that meant.

He'd been too busy with the bodies, ignoring the minds.

Here, the minds were exceptional. The bodies weren't too bad, either. Pity they were on the wrong side.

That got a smile on her face.

"Maybe I will," Mila replied with her own leer.

Javier doubted it would be anything more than a roll in the hay. Women suddenly becoming besotted and seeing the error of their ways after a good romp was a male power fantasy that only happened in books. Mila might be more involved and acrobatic than some women, but it would be raw sex.

Not life changing.

He nodded as a rain check and turned to Zhenya, assuming that she'd be sizing him up as tonight's dessert.

Beautiful in that classical way that was symmetry. Pretty blue eyes. Cute nose. And big tits. Hips meant to be grabbed while dancing. Or *dancing*.

Not as sleek and athletic as Hajna, but probably not into tango, either.

She studied him from close enough that he could have leaned in and stolen a kiss. If he wanted to risk being bitten.

Mila, at least, looked to have some passion hidden under her cool exterior.

Zhenya, from here, looked more like a woman he'd once heard described as the queen of ice and darkness.

Deadly cold, all the way down.

And Javier knew WAY better than to think that he had a magical penis capable of melting her.

Be more worried his dick would freeze solid and break off.

Still, amazingly beautiful. But then, so were some of the classic statues done by Hellenic sculptors eight thousand years ago. They were probably warmer, too.

"So you want to make a statement at *Surayya*?" he asked, mostly to see what story her eyes told. "What's the most valuable target we could get away with?"

Also a trap, but one for her foot to step into, rather than him and his dick.

Dream too big and you might not be able to pull it off. Dream too small and you might relegate yourself down a league in front of someone supposedly playing elite ball.

Her eyes got calculating.

"How do you feel about art?" she countered.

He shrugged.

"Portable value, if done correctly," he replied. "Bethany is my expert when it comes to that sort of thing."

He nodded down to his librarian, watching Zhenya turn. Bethany looked up from her conversation with the Witch Doctor and got his nod, but no words followed either direction.

"I've noticed that you keep a number of women around you, Navarre," Zhenya said when she turned back. "A harem, perhaps?"

"Eye candy," he lied breezily. "All of them are pretty smart, but having babes easy on the eyes makes it all the better. I can do that when I'm in charge."

He specifically didn't draw their attention to Hadiiye. Best if they thought of *his women* as pretty, instead of measuring them on a scale of deadly competence like Javier did. That would give away too much of the game.

At least today.

Still, both Zhenya and Mila nodded. Like they'd just lowered him a whole peg in their overall estimation.

Anything to confuse and distract them.

High stakes poker.

Deadly pots.

"There's a museum on *Surayya*," Kovalev took up her narrative a moment later. "On the outskirts of the capital, not that the city is all that impressive. But there's money. Quite a lot of it, from a few families that managed to build a narrow social pyramid with themselves at the peak."

She paused there, waiting for him to nod.

He did. Probably a company town, from the implications. One family who owned the main factory. And had the money to own the bank. And the bankers. And the politicians. And anybody else important.

Laws would favor them to the exclusion of the everyday people. Rather like *Valadris*, as it existed today.

Exactly the sort of place a Robin Hood gambit like his would want to nail if he was all about public relations.

"Assholes?" he asked, mostly to see her opinion of the family.

"First water," she said, comparing them to the finest diamonds.

Javier hated them already.

Almost as much as he hated Kovalev and her entire culture.

Almost.

Two birds, one stone?

Or rather, two sets of assholes, one terrible warlord?

He'd done crazier things in his time.

"How portable is their wealth?" Navarre-the-killer asked. "We talking paintings easily pulled off walls, or statuary that might break if not handled with infinite delicacy before the reward?"

Again, double entendres. Lots of things worked better if you took time and patience, instead of just bulling ahead. The rewards were much better.

"Some on walls," she nodded. "Some objects that could be taken out of cabinets and put into carriers one person could haul. Jewelry and the like, some of it ancient."

The way she said the word suggested handmade in the times before industry, back on *Earth* itself. Today, you could program one of Suvi's dumber cousins to make something with that same, infinite patience, then have ten thousand copies kicked out, each identical.

In an era of *Sentient* manufacturing precision, human artisans became valuable for the ability to lord it over your friends that you had *artists on staff.*

The Medicis, in ancient Italy during the Renaissance, for example.

"Hard to fence later?" he asked.

In the old days, you might melt down precious metals for specie value. Separate stones to sell.

Today, those *Sentient* factories could spin the specie back up. Make new stones perfectly from raw materials.

The artist was the value. Especially when you could mine gold and other inert metals from asteroid fields.

"We have connections," Kovalev purred. "Folks who might even dislike Surayyan society enough to enjoy the deal."

He nodded. Stacia was close and filming, but he doubted that she'd caught that hint. Maybe Suvi could wash it out of the ambient sound later.

More conversation ended, however, when somebody delivered him what looked like a kilogram of prime rib on a hubcap.

Fattening him up for the slaughter?

PART 8

Javier noted that the pirate scum and villainy at the lower tables had all eaten then bailed, heading off to whatever private parties and crap they did before leaving on a raid in the morning.

Personally, he'd have gone for a quieter evening of reading. Maybe a decaf tea with a little tequila in it and a good book.

But he was also a decade or two older than a lot of those yahoos. Older than even Mila, if he was judging wrinkles and sprouts of gray hair correctly where they peeked out from that turban.

He'd learned the value of not pushing to collapse and exhaustion, because he wasn't young enough to get up in the morning wearing the same uniform as last night to stumble to work, maybe still wearing the bracelet the club put on him.

Food was gone. First dessert as well. Nothing exotic. A kind of bread pudding lighter on rum than he made them, but still tasty.

The top table was still full. That was it.

"If we're going to fly off to some target in twelve hours or so, I need to talk to my people in orbit," Javier announced in a conversational voice. "Clear everything with them so they don't panic at you flying up to meet them without me aboard. Twitchy, ya know."

"Come with me," Zhenya said, climbing up off the bench.

That was a general signal, as the others stood as well.

Zhenya had heels that put her at his height. He figured that might be another tell, if she had physicality issues to deal with. Reminded him of the tall killer in his shadow, until Djamila had gotten over herself for and at *Shangdu*.

"Mila, you get everything set for the morning," Zhenya continued. "We'll launch an hour after dawn."

Javier watched the shorter, heavier woman nod and begin acting like a proper First Officer. Something he'd seen, but never really accomplished. Witch Doctor, Afia, and Bethany went with her. As did Stacia and Suvi.

Zhenya started walking. He fell in behind her, far enough back to watch her ass move. It was a great ass.

A glance back confirmed that Hadiiye was trailing in deadly silence.

As she did.

Zhenya got to a chamber and opened it before she realized that he wasn't alone.

"Not you," she said, looking up at the looming Hadiiye.

"Where he goes, I go," the giant growled down to the lowly folks around her.

Zhenya had a moment of pure, unbridled rage flash across her eyes as Javier watched, then got control of it.

Control freak. He added it to the list of buttons to push later.

"Oh?" Zhenya sneered. "Did you want to join us?"

Lots of ways to answer that and stay in character as a bodyguard.

Javier doubted that the pirate was expecting Hadiiye's dismissive laugh.

"I wouldn't fuck him with your dick, lady," Hadiiye replied.

Dead honest, too. They'd mostly gotten over themselves, but there were still hard lines in their relationship.

Zhenya looked at him. Javier shrugged.

"Hired the best," he offered. "Shouldn't really argue with her expertise on a subject."

"Fine," Zhenya snapped, turning and stepping through the door.

Her suite, obviously.

Nice, too.

Better furniture in a front room that felt like a salon, with a small office desk in one corner. A few paintings on the wall that had bright colors. He wasn't enough art critic to judge past that.

Open door to a hallway. Probably a couple more offices or bedrooms, plus a common bath, like he had, with a main sleeping chamber at the back. Again, like his a few corridors away, but more lived in.

Zhenya moved to the desk while Hadiiye took a spot close to the front door that happened to have her facing directly down the corridor, in case an ambush was waiting.

Javier had known dumber people in his time.

He followed Zhenya at a respectful distance. Came to rest as she pulled out a comm and handed it to him.

"Your ship is on channel eleven," she said, professional again, instead of angry.

Not as much fun as the flirty woman she'd been at dinner. Hopefully, he'd find a way to dial that back in later.

Shame to come all this way and screw it up at this stage. He even had a plan.

The pirate babe watched him as he played with the gadget.

"*Excalibur*, this is Navarre," he said when he got there.

"Go ahead, Captain," Suvi replied instantly in her excited, young Yeoman voice.

Probably waking Zakhar and a few others up to listen in. Piet should have had bridge duty, if he had the time right in his head.

"Roust that lazy bum Sokolov and get him on the line," Navarre groused now.

"Stand by."

Javier stood by.

"This is Sokolov," Zakhar answered a moment later.

They didn't bother with code words on this run, because he had the Suvi Probe occasionally chatting with herself on the ship, once she'd confirmed that the locals had no equipment to detect her signal.

How many pirate organizations really understood signals encryption standards, anyway?

"An hour after sunrise, this whole mob is taking off," Navarre explained grandly. "We're going with them and headed to a place called *Surayya*, where you'll sit in orbit and keep the ticks off our backs."

"Very good, sir," Zakhar replied in a neutral voice, all characters in a Kabuki at this point. "And where will you be?"

"Flying aboard the Second-in-Command's assault ship," Navarre said. "Taking most of my crew, but you'll need to put Smith on the ground to transport Burakgazi and Durbin up to you at local dawn."

"Understood, sir," Zakhar said. "Are there other orders?"

"Nothing at present," Navarre announced. "Be ready to go tomorrow."

Javier cut the line and handed the device back to Kovalev with a warm smile. She took it and put it on the desk, then gave Hadiiye a hard once-over like a side of frozen meat.

Didn't want to have an audience, did we? Pity.

Javier had never suffered that sort of performance anxiety.

A few good drunken orgies along the way and you realized that everyone else was just as nervous.

He took a slow, measured step towards Kovalev. Got her attention centered back on him, without getting close enough to touch.

She could still punch him if she wanted. Not even the first woman in the room to do *that*.

Kovalev let her attention be distracted. Javier took a moment to ogle her like he had Vinogradov at dinner.

One should always appreciate a beautiful woman who wanted to be noticed.

And Zhenya Kovalev was beautiful, whatever else she might also be.

He waited. She was in command around here, so she should be issuing orders. Or something.

Plus, woman, so she should be the one asking. Or not.

He was just a visitor. A Johnny-come-lately with a big warship and a bigger reputation.

As it were.

Kovalev turned back to Hadiiye.

"She follows you everywhere?" the woman asked.

"And never talks afterwards," he nodded, just to see if they'd hit a hard stop for her.

Interesting, but you never knew where somebody's lines were until you hit them.

Frequently, at full speed.

Kovalev turned back to him.

"Are you as good as you present?" she asked, voice loosening up some finally.

"Depends on what you have in mind," he countered. "I can stay. I can go back to my quarters. Your call."

Probably a novel experience for a woman like that. She'd come up through the ranks, from what small talk he'd gotten at dinner. Been a better pilot, a better killer, a better pirate than any of the rest, until folks had to give way.

He liked that in a woman. Pity they had to meet like this.

Javier held out a hand. She took it after a moment. Probably never been treated like a lady, either.

Either just one of the boys, or it would turn into more power games naked. Those were far more common than most people realized.

Just another form of social combat.

He took a half step, finally entering her space.

Something jarred loose, because she took the other half step and was touching him, chest to chest.

"And after this raid?" Kovalev asked.

"Once we're done at *Surayya*, I'm back to *Valadris*, then on to my next mission," he said. "Unless I get an invitation to return to *Syntha* at some future date."

He left that dangling. Open-ended, like they might coordinate vacations occasionally. Peers, when he doubted that she had any men under her smart enough to let her be in charge without thinking with their dicks.

Like most of the men he knew. Occasionally including himself.

At least he had a cast of smart women around him that didn't have to genuflect before his glory.

Kovalev considered it for a long moment. Then she nodded at him. Added a challenging smile.

"Okay, hotshot," she said. "Let's see what you got."

He could almost hear Djamila's eyeroll from here, but this was all part of the mission.

Even the beautiful women.

SURAYYA

PART 1

Zakhar sat on his command throne and pondered the planet in the distance. *Neu Berne* had built the space for the captain at the center of a ring of stations facing in, with a second ring around the outside of the large, round chamber facing the walls.

He was elevated above, on a gimbal that let him spin to face any of his Centurions as he needed. Silly design, but he'd only stolen the ship, not redesigned it to be more like he'd prefer.

He'd make do.

"Piet, Suvi, talk to me," he announced, looking down on his Pilot and First Officer.

"*Surayya* was originally terraformed in the third wave," Piet replied after a glance down to where Suvi appeared on a small screen in front of him, like she did Zakhar. "Like a lot of those worlds, ignored for several centuries while things got settled, then forgotten because of some of the wars and other issues in those days. Didn't have a large, permanent human settlement until starting around three hundred years ago.

Small even today by most standards, but strongly centralized around a single city, with rings of farms and ranches ranging outwards from that."

"Trade?" Zakhar asked.

"Largely export of raw goods, Captain," Suvi replied. "The economy is still too small to support itself industrially, but slowly improving and industrializing as a small number of factories are added every few years for various goods. All of them appear to be owned by a single family unit. A clan, I think you would classify them, with marriages that don't fall far outside of a narrow group. Like European aristocracy in the early Industrial Age on Earth."

"Defenses we've been able to detect?" Zakhar pressed.

That was all he really cared about. Javier had only given him the basics. Afia and Bethany, watching from the outer ring, hadn't been able to add much.

Fortunately, his own paranoia was sufficient to have folks research things like that and keep sailing directions as up to date as possible.

"Two squadrons of one-man fighter ships that appear to have been an early generation design from the Great War," Piet replied. "Total of twenty-six, but I doubt that they can get all of them flying these days. If we see twenty, I'd be surprised. Still, purpose-built craft, rather than junkyard models welded together, so probably worth two to three times their weight in pirates. Nothing at all that is a risk to us."

"I presume Javier still expects us to hover in place over the city while they hit it," Zakhar said. "Not go hunting. Still, keep all transponders and identification signals off until we leave the system permanently, Suvi. They might recognize us, but I don't ever plan to fly this way again."

"Continuing, Captain," she said.

"Mary-Elizabeth, how good are the horde?"

His Gunner was a lot of things. A good judge of pirates was among them.

"They got numbers," she replied with a sarcastic drawl. "That's always good for something. Maybe a handful of them actually know more than flying and shooting. Most would wash out of piloting school with anybody who wasn't desperate."

"Plague of locusts, M-E," Zakhar laughed. "Two hundred of them against twenty defenders isn't even remotely fair, so they can do things even here. Without us, it would be much different."

"Captain, I'm picking up the first alert signals from the planetary defense network," Suvi overrode everything. "They've picked up the ships down in closer to the planet finally and are starting to react."

"Alert me if anybody locks onto us with a weapons system of any kind," Zakhar replied. "Your guns are clear, but hold things for defensive fire only at present."

"Acknowledged," Suvi replied.

"Piet, start us in," Zakhar ordered.

Time to see what kind of game the pirates had planned.

PART 2

Stacia had filmed the Vinogradov woman and her small crew over several days on the flight from *Syntha* to *Surayya*. And noted when Navarre shared the woman's bunk for a few hours, but not longer than that. If it was anything like her own hammock, Stacia honestly couldn't see what you could accomplish with two people.

Even in zero gravity, you needed to be strapped to things so you didn't fly off. Her bag wouldn't even hold two people.

Still, Stacia kept her opinions to herself and filmed Vinogradov mostly. Sometimes Navarre, when he nodded to her that he had something to say. Frequently, leading questions that Vinogradov would answer in ways that told Stacia how much information someone was feeding those pirates.

And how much of it came from *Valadris*, which was the part she really cared about.

Supposedly, Afia and Bethany had a list of names, but they'd split off at the start and Stacia hadn't even had a chance for a quick goodbye kiss.

Had to be professional. Shoot your footage and spend your time scripting it into a narrative that could be played back later on the evening news. And in courtrooms.

Vinogradov was piloting. Her ship was a long tube of steel and other materials, with most of the wiring below the single deck. Three days in zero gravity had been educational, but Stacia had managed to eat and go to the restroom without too much trouble.

Two long sleeping chambers down the sides, with extra hammocks hung until you were cheek-in-jowl with folks. Or slept in shifts, which she'd taken to doing.

Common space for food, entertainment, and just waiting around. Right now filled with three of Vinogradov's people in an uneasy alliance with all of the Dragoon's killers, as everyone checked weapons and engaged in the sorts of crude locker room talk Stacia had learned to ignore.

None of it was aimed at her, after Iqbal and Demyan had pointed out to the men that she wasn't interested.

She floated forward, pulled along by Suvi's probe, which was a great way to travel around this ship.

Navarre in the copilot's chair, next to Vinogradov. Stacia let go and grabbed the door frame.

"Is it okay to film while you're making the run?" she asked politely. "The probe can sit in the corner for good face shots, and be out of your way."

Vinogradov looked over at Navarre and got a shrug.

"Go ahead," the woman said in a surly voice that now had to deal with *one more thing*.

Stacia would keep it easy from here.

"Probe. Access Command Node," Stacia began. Suvi was good about waiting for orders, then understanding them better than Stacia framed the words at times. "Move to the forward left corner, reverse yourself into the notch, and begin filming."

"Acknowledged," the woman said in her mechanical voice.

Stacia waited. Outside the window, the horizon was coming up as the ship started to dive. If she understood things correctly, Captain Kovalev was already ahead somewhere, in a four-crew ship, leading. Her as pilot. A turret gunner. A navigator who doubled as squadron communications, and a fourth that concentrated on food and cleanup. Butler, maybe, so the others could be on duty and fighting at any moment.

"Madame Vinogradov, since most of my viewers will have never launched a pirate raid against an unsuspecting world, could you walk us through things as you go?" Stacia asked in the most banal tone she could manage while about to kill innocent people. "Don't worry about gaps. I'll edit those out later."

Vinogradov again looked over at Navarre, like she didn't believe that this shit was really happening.

Trick's on you, babe. This was all his idea in the first place.

But Stacia didn't say anything.

"We've come out of that last jump only covering a short distance," Vinogradov began narrating. Confessing. Something. "All the ships are currently starting to cluster, but not too tightly. Partly, there are no defenders in the skies to threaten us at present. Partly because we need space to maneuver this many vessels. We'll attack in a spiraling dive, rather than a horizontal glide, because it is faster to the ground, and every minute we give those people to prepare is that much longer someone has to arm themselves. Easier if we just overwhelm them at first, both intellectually as well as psychologically. Get them to just stand around. Usually, we only have to kill a few people to get our point across. *Surayya* might be different, because they have a fairly large police force down there. Teams have been assigned to strafe the police headquarters and suppress them from organizing, while others will land on the edge of town and assault the museum that is our target."

"Is this normal for you?" Stacia pressed, letting herself take nine long steps back in her head, away from what was happening.

Navarre had given her no words, but seemed confident that the raid would go badly at some point.

"Not the strafing part," Vinogradov acknowledged. "Usually, we just buzz somebody to let them know we're serious and here in large numbers. That's generally sufficient to make them behave while we rob them blind."

Stacia ground her teeth, happy that nobody could see her right now except Suvi. She could cut and frame these shots later, considering what her face probably looked like.

"Will all two hundred ships land, then?" she continued her interview.

"Probably three-quarters," was the answer. "A few need to remain at low altitude against ground-based attack craft, since we have your ship protecting us up in orbit."

Definitely chopping that part out. Assuming that Navarre and Sokolov weren't pulling a fast one on Stacia now and had decided to join the pirate women.

Navarre/Aritza didn't look like a man who would be led astray by his penis. And Sokolov was more or less married to the Dragoon, though that was part of a larger poly cluster in ways she didn't need to explore for this documentary.

Not as complicated as Aritza, though, which was good.

"And the museum?" Stacia pressed forward, marching in her mind as if to her own hanging.

"Someplace we've wanted to hit for a while," Vinogradov laughed. "But it required too many moving parts to pull off. Navarre helps. Stand by, atmospheric turbulence is going to get heavier. Move to the jumpseat and strap yourself in."

Stacia pushed off and did so. Not that comfortable, but she supposed that gravity was going to take hold soon, and the ship was pointed more or less straight down like a falling arrow at this point.

Better safe.

Outside, the windows started to glow with the heat of reentry. That was fine. Stacia was about out of questions.

Most of the interesting bits would occur on the ground.

For evil or good.

PART 3

Djamila had taken the time to study the planetary information available about *Surayya* and had Del bring her and her team temperate climate gear when he'd come for Afia and Bethany. Nothing as fancy as Hadiiye normally wore, but that worked in her favor, as she was in speckled gray and tan that would be hard to focus on at any distance. Same for her team.

While it wasn't the first time they'd done something like this, it had been a while. Not since they'd stole the Land Leviathan for the team. Not that she'd let them slack one bit in their training. If anything, they'd all ramped it up a full notch since then.

Like they expected to be doing crazier things, having finally joined Javier in his crusade to save the galaxy.

"Final approach," the Vinogradov woman said from up front.

Djamila had taken command of the other three gunslingers, at least until everyone was on the ground. At that point, she presumed that Vinogradov or Kovalev would issue contrary orders.

How Javier planned to betray everything was the final piece that Djamila was watching for. And the when.

She had no doubts that it was coming. She'd come to know the man's face well enough by now.

Poker player, which was something she'd never understood. However, she could watch his eyes get perfectly flat and emotionless when things got serious. Back at the table, sitting on a hand that could win big, if he bluffed and finessed it just right.

Yes, he had that look in his eyes.

Djamila turned to the oldest of Vinogradov's goons. She'd barely rate the man as a qualified infantry trooper, but it wasn't her army.

"You're her bodyguards when we hit the ground?" she confirmed.

"That's right," the man nodded. "Normally, she's in the second wave for something like this, bringing up the ground troopers, once some of the pilots shut down their sleds and join us."

"Fine," Djamila replied. "You stay with her then. We'll move up with the first wave."

"Really?" he asked. Sounded like he expected them to let the others take the risk.

Normal junior enlisted thinking.

"There's no Land Leviathan around here for us to steal, but we're capable," she said.

The man fell silent, as did his two cohorts. They'd previously asked and been told about that mission. In Djamila's mind, it was still one of the best ground assaults anyone had pulled off in recent memory. Possibly living memory, not counting Suvi and her kind.

"Landing imminent," Vinogradov said over the speakers.

Everyone grabbed hold of something stable and waited.

The ship landed fairly conventionally, coming in at a fast glide, then stalling and settling. Aft, three thrusters on pylons left space for the rear to clamshell open into a loading ramp. Given the available volume, Djamila could see important cargo normally being stashed back here, except that adding all these bodies and supplies had filled a lot of it.

There were a few other ships with big cargo bays available. Djamila wasn't in charge of logistics for packing loot. That was Galal's specialization, when he wasn't being a Grenadier.

Djamila nodded to her people and moved to the rear. Weapons were live, but Vinogradov's three were in front of them. It wasn't that Djamila didn't trust the woman.

She didn't. She also didn't trust the situation.

She did trust that Javier had a con job going that would be another one spoken of in hushed tones between people sitting in quiet back rooms.

He had that sort of impact on lives.

They landed.

Djamila nodded and the one trooper opened the hatch, letting her people hit the ground and establish a perimeter. Djamila moved to one side and waited for Javier and Vinogradov to emerge.

Didn't take long. The woman wore a pistol on her hip, with a pulse carbine slung across her back where it was absolutely useless in any sort of engagements. Plus, the carbine barrel would hardly improve your engagement range over the pistol itself.

Djamila had upgraded Hadiiye's rig to a pair of long-barrel pulsars that probably ranged better than the carbine. Pinpoint deadly at two hundred meters, at least in her hands.

Javier had the gear Djamila had assigned him. Interchangeable power packs with everyone else not firing slugs or explosives. The sword in case he needed to look threatening or knight someone along the way.

Djamila qualified him as last among her people, and probably still better than at least two of Vinogradov's troopers. But then, Stacia might be more dangerous than those two. She'd be happier when they were far enough away as to only be random threats.

Vinogradov studied Djamila in combat gear as she emerged, Javier in her wake.

"I'm planning on heading in first," Djamila announced. She nodded to Stacia, just now coming out into the late morning sun. "Stacia, you can wait here and send the probe, or join us and leave it here."

"I'd like to see it happen in real time," Javier announced.

Everyone turned to Vinogradov. There was an air of challenge hanging. Did she want to hang back and organize things while the others were possibly shooting? Or dive into the thick of things?

Vinogradov turned to her three and sorted the leader from the fools.

"You two remain here and guard the ship," the woman ordered. "You find Zhenya and let her know what we're up to."

Everyone nodded and Djamila set her pathfinders into motion.

Edge of town. The ship had landed in a field and scared off a small herd of cattle, at least for now. If there was a bull, he might be a problem later.

Other ships had landed haphazardly around them, stretched out backwards from a large building that looked like a shipping container with a single clocktower on the…south corner. Men and a few women were all moving towards the building that Djamila assumed was the museum about to be robbed.

Sascha and Hajna moved at a jog. Not that they needed to run interference up front, but because their job was to scout.

"Testing audio," Djamila said.

"Six and zero," Hajna replied.

Perfect signal. No static.

Others spoke up and Djamila was satisfied. For now. The pirates didn't seem to have personal comms, relying on word of mouth or radios in ships to talk.

Stupid, when assaulting a ground target.

But nobody had hired her to run this operation.

She paused, waiting and locking eyes with a deadly serious Javier as they started into motion.

Djamila corrected herself.

Javier had hired her for a specific purpose.

She simply didn't know who he needed killed yet.

PART 4

Javier focused on being Navarre-the-killer. That rude, vicious, *MEAN* son of a bitch who made people piss their boots when he was around.

Or something like that.

Mila had been fun in the sack, once she stopped trying to be tough all the time. Ticklish, if you took the time to look. Never gonna make a housefrau, but he could see a few choice decision points in her past where she might have been another Zakhar Sokolov. Or a successful corporate exec somewhere.

Today, they were about to rob a museum.

And not even a caper, damn it.

Just another smash and grab job.

Amateur hour.

He stretched his stride enough that Hadiiye's impossible legs would be comfortable. And the rest would have to half-jog to keep up.

O'er yonder, he could see a mob of goobers in the parking lot, milling around as they tried to find their own asses with both hands, a map, and a flashlight.

Looked like the map was winning.

He identified Zhenya Kovalev in the middle, counting noses and getting people psyched up to execute a frontal assault.

At least he didn't have to worry about cops, as a pair of fighters zinged by overhead, explosions in the distance where they'd hit police headquarters again. Place was already burning, but Javier understood that juvenile delinquent drive to blow shit up.

He shouldered a skinny punk out of his way and walked up to Kovalev.

"Anybody hit the building yet?" he asked.

She scowled at him.

"About to," she replied.

Javier looked around at the mismatch of weapons and gunners. Damned near every kind, make, and model of personal-portable firearm or blaster he could think of off the top of his head. And more than a few he'd have to ask to identify.

He felt like being a shit. A bigger shit.

The king-badass of shits.

He turned to Hadiiye. Scowled up at the woman in her guise as the Ballerina of Death.

"Stun weapons only," he ordered. "Rapid assault. Prisoners so we can interrogate them as to whatever I want to know later. Questions?"

She paused, digesting, then turned to her Gunbunnies.

"Galal, you have the front door," she said. "Assume they've managed to lock it."

That one nodded.

Then the seven of them were off at damned near a dead run across the parking lot. Javier watched a few of the more ambitious pirates start out in their wake, but piracy didn't lend one's self to four-hundred-meter wind sprints in full gear.

They fell behind quickly. A few even tried to keep up, but most stopped after about twenty meters and looked back.

He hadn't even tried. Instead, Javier started walking, nodding to Kovalev and Vinogradov to join him on his saunter.

Something like seventy-five or one hundred folks went with him.

Javier paused and looked around for Suvi's unblinking eyeball staring back at him.

"All of you hold your fire," he snarled in an uglier voice than the situation really required, but he was making a point. On film. For eternity, as it were. "My team will neutralize the guards, then you can go in. In fact, best if most of you put away your guns now so you don't accidentally shoot anyone friendly. Hadiiye might stop her assault and hunt you down if you did that."

A few looked like they wanted to get pissy with him on that point, until Galal put a rifle grenade into the main doors of the museum with the sort of precision those lunatics preferred, followed by the rest charging through, firing as they went.

They hadn't even broken stride.

A few mouths fell open as they watched real professionals work. Javier liked to tease those men, but he'd honestly never known another small arms unit of that caliber.

The scary part was when Djamila talked about her old unit in the *Neu Berne* Assault Marines, whose logo Javier wore as part of his costume. If she was to be believed—and she rarely lied about such things—then those folks made hers today look like amateur pikers.

Not that he wanted to upgrade. The universe was better with *Neu Berne* no longer a threat to anyone.

One look at that museum should tell you that.

PART 5

Djamila was first through the door. Sascha and Hajna would be last, then start scouting, but Javier had wanted a splashy entrance, followed by all the guards being safely captured instead of being killed by fools.

Part of the legend of Navarre.

Two heads popped up from behind a receptionist's desk, intending to fire at her.

She stunned both and kept moving forward.

Someone on her right—probably Iqbal—put a stun grenade down a hallway with a double strike of blinding light followed by thunder.

"Two teams, split!" she yelled, heading towards the main hallway back into the interior.

More folks back there, ducked into doorways or behind trashcans. Hardly protected. Easy to spot. Not much of a threat.

Her Hogan's Alley, back in *Excalibur*, set to a rating Two, perhaps. If she wanted Javier to qualify for something.

Djamila did Eights on average days. Ten when she felt like challenging the gods themselves.

Beam fire and one more stun grenade, then there was nobody conscious in sight that wasn't hers.

"Pathfinders," Djamila called quietly. "Scout and report."

Sascha appeared in the corner of her eye, then went down the hall like a bit of smoke in a hard breeze. Most people could not move silently at that speed. Most people weren't pathfinders.

Djamila held where she was and waited for her experts to report. Singles they could take themselves. It would only be clusters where they called for help.

Djamila glanced back and nodded. Everything under control, with Iqbal tying up the guards in sight while Tom and Helmfried dragged more bodies over.

Navarre appeared at the outer hatch with his plague of locusts. Paused there until she waved him in.

She'd been expecting fools, but Navarre had distracted the pirates at the perfect moment. Djamila's team might be able to clear the place right on the first pass, without needing meaningless firefights in hallways that damaged loot.

"Status?" Navarre asked as he and the two women came close.

Most of the pirates were still outside.

"Breach secured," Djamila replied, already in full combat mode and not coming back from that for a while. "Scouts penetrating. Prisoners there."

"Anybody shooting back right now, pathfinders?" he asked.

Both women laughed over the comm.

Navarre nodded and moved to the desk. Djamila watched him pick up a handset and do something. Turned out to be the intercom.

"This facility has been captured," his voice emerged from speakers overhead a moment later. "The guards are safe as prisoners. They are unhurt, except for being stunned. I have no reason to kill you, so it would be easier for everyone if you surrendered now and came to the front where we can tie you up and keep you out of the way while we rob the place."

Djamila noted that he hadn't invoked his legend by using his name.

She assumed the triple-cross was imminent and placed herself in such a way that she had the best angle to start taking down pirates outside.

Navarre put the headset down and walked over to Kovalev with a grin. At least he was smart enough not to cross in front of her, in case she needed to start shooting.

"That's it?" Kovalev asked.

"That's it," Navarre agreed. "I don't kill people unless they needed killing. Nobody who works here qualifies, so they can all go home safe tonight when we're done. Give it five minutes and then you're moving things with hand trucks and carts."

"Is this how you normally operate?" Vinogradov growled.

"Patience and delicacy," Navarre turned to her next. "I seem to remember that it works wonders, instead of bulling ahead."

Djamila would have lost a bet that the hard woman could blush like that, but Vinogradov did. But then, every woman who had spent time in the sack with Javier had good things to say about the man. And as Dragoon, then or now, she'd have bounced him off a bulkhead if a woman had complained about the sex.

Apparently, he'd worked his magic on those two, as well, because Kovalev blushed as well.

"I have movement headed your way," Hajna said. "Hands in the air people! Walk nice, be nice, and nobody gets hurt today!"

Djamila nodded to Iqbal and everyone got into positions. She turned to the two pirate queens and nodded, then walked around them to deal with the men outside. Almost all men. Eight to one, give or take.

Pigeons to her hawk.

"Put your guns away!" she called in a voice that echoed off nearby ships a few moments later. "Prisoners are surrendering. In fact, why don't you make yourselves useful and start driving your ground vehicles down here. Or hotwire some of the ones in the parking lot so we can haul things faster. Every minute on the ground is that much more prepared they are when we leave. Move it, people!"

Helped that they were used to taking orders from a woman. Most of them started into motion immediately.

Djamila watched for a moment, then turned and noticed Stacia standing four meters away with her camera in hand and her jaw so far open it might be painful. Certainly, she could catch a lot of flies.

Djamila couldn't help herself. Too many years around Javier.

She winked at the camera and turned to walk back inside.

More prisoners were arriving and being quickly frisked and tied up. Demyan was marching them outside, where they had a shady spot to sit out of the way, while others started carrying some of the unconscious guards out and adding them to the mix.

She was back aboard the Land Leviathan, when Javier had insisted on capturing everyone when her first intention had been a complete bloodbath.

But Navarre didn't work that way.

"Facility is secured," Sascha announced a few moments later. "Back fire doors are locked and a couple of folks bolted that way, but they are not looking back. All civilians from garb."

Djamila nodded and went to see how Javier was going to handle whatever surprise he had in mind next.

PART 6

Stacia had honestly thought she'd been prepared for Captain Navarre and his deadly gun moll Hadiiye.

Instead, she would have nightmares for the rest of her life, actually watching this unfold. Filming it even.

Military precision. Elite training. Non-lethal fire. Prisoners handled with delicacy.

Everything that Captain Kovalev and her Pirate Horde were not. It was almost like he was rubbing their faces in the fact that they weren't as good.

Did the man have a death wish, to do this in front of so many armed lunatics?

Then the Dragoon walked out and issued orders to the entire horde. And those men obeyed her.

Shit.

Stacia followed the woman back inside, camera running in case something happened. Suvi would also be filming, so they made it a point to remain opposite each other as much as possible.

Still, shit.

"Captain Kovalev," Navarre said politely. "Thanks for letting my people kick in the door. I think we should get out of your way now and let your people go to town. This is far more in your expertise than mine, and I'm pretty sure we'd look like fools, trying to guess which pieces were valuable and which pretty. Especially considering the research you've done."

He nodded deep enough to almost be a bow, then stepped back, watched them, then turned and headed to the door.

Hadiiye and her people followed. WITHOUT A SINGLE WORD BEING SAID!

Stacia had no idea which group to film right now. Then her instincts bit her on the ass.

"Probe. Access Command Node," she called. "Attach to Mila Vinogradov and capture footage of her and her teams as they work."

Stacia stayed close to Kovalev. She could follow one woman and hear orders and conversations. Everything today was evidence that would stand up in any court of law anywhere. Even after Navarre and his ship left.

And he'd only committed heavy vandalism, at the end of the day. All the people inside safely captured. Nobody hurt any more than falling down after being stunned. Moved out of the way and put where they could watch, but nothing more.

Kovalev took a long moment that felt to Stacia like a hard look in the mirror in the morning. Then she shook herself once and a new deadliness came into her eyes.

Stacia happened to be perfectly aligned to watch it, and film it.

Those eyes promised death to someone. Stacia had a pretty good idea who.

That might be why he'd left the building. Did he know what was coming?

Yes. Did he know when?

Shit, probably.

How far ahead had he and the others gamed this out?

And how much risk was she herself in? She was alone with them, with Suvi off watching Vinogradov work.

Stacia carefully swallowed past a suddenly dry tongue and wondered what was next.

CAPTAIN NAVARRE

PART 1

Zakhar studied the plot. He owned orbital space above *Surayya*. Flying a First-Rate Galleon in this age did that, when so many nations had beached or even broken up their old warships a generation ago.

Peace benefits, they'd said.

Things that let a pirate Strike Corvette run rampant.

Excalibur was a *wee bit meaner* than a mere Strike Corvette.

"Captain, I am detecting launches from the ground commensurate with orbital attack fighters," Suvi announced.

He nodded. About freaking time, too. Hopefully, somebody around here was getting fired when all this was done. He'd begun to wonder if the pirates had penetrated the local constabulary forces and managed to neutralize them from the inside with a good bribe or some juicy blackmail.

They should have launched twenty minutes ago.

He was *professionally* offended.

"How secure are their communications?" he asked.

Around him, everyone jolted out of their daydreams and began punching buttons.

Showtime.

"I could probably crack it in roughly three minutes of dedicated effort, sir," Suvi replied.

He nodded again. So much power at his fingertips.

And he had a niece he could spoil.

"Suvi, withdraw all attention except for monitoring on your shards to crack their systems. I want to talk to them without others listening," he said. Then Zakhar pushed the big red button on his armrest. The *Voice of God* button. "All hands, stand by for entirely mechanical operations until further notice. You are on your own."

Heh.

He made a note to do this more often, just so nobody got lazy and expected Suvi to handle everything. He doubted that they'd slide that far, but better safe than sorry.

Piet certainly woke up and started doing things. Normally, he offered her suggestions like a First Officer overseeing a young Yeoman learning the ropes. And Suvi had told him how much better she'd gotten, learning from the man.

Mary-Elizabeth leaned back and cracked her knuckles with a maniacal laughter that he hadn't heard in a while.

Afia rolled her eyes at everyone and everything, while she and Bethany continued to whisper.

Orbital defense forces might and might not be a pain in his ass. That all depended on them. Nothing on his screen suggested a threat to *Excalibur*. Hardly even an annoyance.

And when the pirates lifted off, they wouldn't even rate that highly.

PART 2

Javier nodded as he got outside and most of the pirates traded places with him. Nobody was willing to simply stand guard on the prisoners at this point, so he moved over to stand close to one older woman in nice slacks and blazer that looked like either a senior docent or maybe management.

Either way, a credible witness. That would be useful later.

He smiled at the woman, her looking up at him with a growl on her face that was as yet unvoiced.

"You and your people are safe," he said. "Nobody has been hurt. That's on purpose. Ignore the excessive violence getting you there, because that's just property vandalism and can be repaired."

"And everything you intend to steal, young man?" she managed without any of the profanities he'd been expecting.

"That's Captain Kovalev and her pirate horde from *Syntha*," he replied, watching her eyes get big enough to see the whites. "Could have gone the other way. Again, nothing in this building was yours. If the people who own the place didn't insure it, that sounds like a bad corporate gamble where they overruled their accountants and legal staff. Not my fuckup, lady."

"So you'll just clean the place out and be done with it?" she sneered in that arch way that only an older woman could truly make work.

Javier was impressed.

"No, actually," he said.

Then he squatted down next to her, close enough to smell her perfume and really making her nervous. But he wanted her undivided attention. Most of the staff was too far away to hear what he was about to say. Some of them hadn't woken up fully from the stun.

"I'm going to pull a massive triple-cross on those folks shortly," he murmured in her ear. "But they greatly outnumber me on the ground. I need to get them in the air, feeling awesome and lazy enough that they get stupid. I have reinforcements in orbit right now, setting things up. Scanner logs later will show what happened, but I want you to be able to tell the authorities that it was not a falling out among pirates. That it was an inside job."

"Why?" she demanded after a long moment, in a hard, cold whisper.

"Because I'm Captain Navarre," he said, watching her face blanch. "Yeah, that guy. Because some folks from *Byormi* hired me to destroy Captain Kovalev and all her people. You have a front row seat to watch part of it. The rest is coming."

"Aren't you a pirate?" she asked quietly. Confused instead of combative now.

"I'm a killer, lady," Navarre laughed. "All of the folks I've destroyed to date have been pirates. It's all a matter of public relations, and I haven't bothered correcting certain bad assumptions. Today, that's going to change a little, because

I'm on my way out of this entire region of space, so you'll never have to worry about me and my crew again. And you can talk to the short blonde with the camera later. She's going back to *Valadris* with a lot of film footage of all this, shot under the guise of making a documentary about piracy."

"Why?" she repeated.

"Because it needed doing," Javier said. "And nobody else was willing. There is a storm coming, and you don't have too many years to prepare for those winds. Make the most of them."

He stood up and walked away before she could speak. Not much more to say. Word would get out, but it would muddy so many things that folks beyond this region would discount it.

At least for now.

Valadris would hopefully learn. Maybe *Surayya* as well.

Not his problem. As he'd said to folks, he was providing the opportunity. They still had to take it.

Here's a door, you have to kick it in.

Javier looked around and noted the layout.

"Hadiiye," he called, loud enough to get all heads turned his way, instead of just the old woman with the cagey eyes. "Let's move everyone around the side of the building. There should be a break area or something that gets them out of sight of the pirates when they start exiting the building. After all this work, I don't want some jackass opening fire because he's got a gun and no fire discipline."

More shock. The good kind. Folks confused instead of resigned to death.

Djamila and her boys got folks standing while the pathfinders kept watch. Walked them around the corner of the building to a nice little park-like area, surrounded by trees and brush to the point that they'd be invisible. She got them seated in chairs and on benches. More comfortable.

More importantly, safe.

The old woman's scowl was gone. Calculation had replaced it.

Javier nodded.

"Think of all of this as a monumental con job, lady," he told her quietly. "You won't be far off."

PART 3

Suvi watched and scanned. She was also tracking Stacia's camera, both physically by location pings as well as watching a feed from the camera's audio and video feeds.

Kovalev and her people had zero electronic security protocols in place. None. Nothing.

Morons.

Suvi was shocked at how incompetent these people came across, even though it made her job so much easier. But then, she and several of her friends had all retired from the *Concord* Navy, where the training was rigid and intense, intended to turn out sailors worthy of the name.

Most of the folks in scanner range were punks with guns on their best days.

Still, she had a solid hold on things. Javier and Djamila had moved their group around out of sight, hiding all the prisoners and letting Suvi and hopefully Stacia know what was going on. If she was listening and paying attention.

Soon.

For now, Suvi was following the Vinogradov woman

around, ostensibly shooting footage but mostly tracking what was being stolen and adding that to future indictments.

Assuming survivors to haul before a grand jury.

Suvi stayed four meters up and pinged constantly.

Vinogradov walked out of a larger hall and Suvi followed her down a hallway and into a secured area with a lot of gold jewelry on pedestals and displays. Nice stuff, if a little ornate for her tastes.

Suvi wasn't into baroque, but understood that human culture had an annoying tendency to pendulum from simple to *busy* on generational or century scales. Someone around here liked her crap complicated and overly adorned. And definitely a her, from a few pictures on the wall of a matronly figure with some decent plastic surgery around the face to try to look young while showing off many of these pieces.

Showing off her wealth, more likely.

Suvi could fuss and curse in the privacy of her drone, since nobody could hear her but her ship-side self that she sent updates to regularly. Ship-Suvi was also unimpressed.

Then gun butts and fists began smashing into cases. Or trying, only to discover that the glass wasn't anything they could break with their bare hands.

So some idiot fired his gun at a lock.

Fortunately, the ricochet went more or less straight up, embedding in the ceiling tiles rather than hitting anyone. Wouldn't hurt her drone, other than to ping off her skin and into something else.

This was not the room to be playing pinball with humans.

"Cut that shit out!" Vinogradov yelled. "Get the mechanics in here. They have tools for a reason!"

Suvi floated up and stayed out of line of sight as several ijits raced off. More came back. These looked halfway competent.

Okay, maybe three-quarters. One of the men had an impact hammer with some high quality drill bits in place. He leaned into the lock and punched the face off. His partner stepped in when he stepped back, jamming a different bit in from his own hammer, twisting the lock.

Alarms finally started going off. Or maybe just the audible ones.

Suvi assumed hard-wired alarms going downtown to the building these delinquent yahoos had blown up before landing. The cops had other problems than a museum robbery.

She dialed her audio sensors down a few notches, then added a quick routine to wash the alarm out so she could hear everything else ambient.

One by one, the two smarter crooks opened cases and moved on. The punks scooped everything up and started dumping it into briefcases, regardless of how fragile it might be.

But then, they weren't art collectors in anything but the most literal sense today.

Whatever damage occurred wasn't going to really impact the value of the pieces, because they'd either be melted down or sold as stolen anyway.

Still, she wished these fools had more pride in their work.

If you were going to steal something, try not to look like a punk, huh?

She idly considered offering lessons in piracy and theft, but sow's ears and silk purses came to mind.

"Suvi, this is Javier," he suddenly pinged her. "Can you round up Stacia? I need her outside by the ship."

Ah HA!!!

SHOWTIME!

She'd wondered if they were planning to abandon the drone body down here. Wasn't like she wasn't transmitting everything to herself on the ship in real time, once they realized that the pirates weren't listening. Only loss would have been the frame itself, and the time spent tuning it.

Stacia was the problem, because she needed to get out safely.

And that time was now.

Suvi considered her personal fashion, here inside her drone. Her look. Up until now, she'd been in her usual flight cockpit that looked almost exactly like it had on *Mielikki*, back in the before time.

But that was too…staid.

She transformed herself into the four-armed piano-playing version, swapped her green uniform for the hot pink polar bear furs, and dialed up her Red Baron music.

Time to get silly.

PART 4

Stacia had kept a more-than-respectable distance from Kovalev as the woman worked.

Collateral damage kept coming to mind, and she didn't want it to fall on her. Not as grumpy as the pirate queen had gotten over the last fifteen minutes.

Finally processed how bad she had looked, compared to Navarre's strike team?

Something.

Her camera beeped in ways that it hadn't before. She looked down and saw that her diagnostics screen had a message from Suvi.

Navarre requests you join him outside soonest.

Nothing more. Still, it spoke volumes, if everything was coming to a head.

Stacia turned to the nearest pirate. A male, but most of them were.

"Where's the restroom?" she asked.

"Huh?"

"Restroom," she repeated, like he was stupid or something.

He pointed.

Stacia nodded and headed that direction. Kovalev was moving around, but not at a fast pace. Enough that if she took her time in the bathroom, the woman might move deeper into the facility.

Helped that gendered bathrooms seemed deeply ingrained in the pirates. No men in here. Few women with the force in the first place, not counting the Dragoon and her pathfinders.

Stacia took her time. Typed a reply to Suvi.

Potty break then away.

She got a string of smiley faces back that were more like the woman flying the ship than the mechanical device that was pretending to be in the drone.

Stacia emerged from the bathroom and looked around. Nobody in sight, so she turned right and headed towards the front, passing a few pirates headed inwards and falling into a stream headed out with loot.

Paintings literally ripped off the walls from the broken wires on the back. Anvil cases no doubt filled with *objects d'art*. Whatever pirates might find valuable enough to steal instead of breaking.

She filmed as she went, trying to look like a professional, rather than a thief. Or an honest woman surrounded by thieves. Something.

They had guns, and she could still hear occasional explosions in the distance as they flew over the city blowing things up because there was nobody to stop them.

Hopefully, their time was about over.

Stacia moved past the nearer ships. The ones with open bays where folks were stacking and packing like movers. That, at least, they seemed capable of doing in a semi-adult manner.

Hard to steal everything if you can't carry it off.

Finally, she got out past the parking lot. She could see Aritza's party mostly because the Dragoon was so much taller than everyone else.

They were looking this way, but she was still maybe two hundred meters away.

Then the Dragoon drew a pistol and fired it at her.

PART 5

Zhenya looked around when a clock in her head told her that the annoying little blonde with the camera should have been back by now.

Wasn't like she could have gotten lost. This building wasn't that complicated. Just a series of larger and smaller chambers, largely separated by doors or short hallways.

And McNulty should have been back already.

Zhenya sneered at the woman's weakness.

Had a touch of queasiness to finally see what piracy looked like? Wasn't nearly as clean and pretty as filmmakers presented it?

On the one hand, a constant struggle against the authorities on various planets who might not want to pay tribute to keep her at bay. At the other end of the spectrum, people coveting her power and position and working to undermine her or simply kill her and take over the gang.

Like she'd done.

Mila was not a threat. Not that many people would follow her if she made her move. And she seemed to understand that she could have what power she had as Zhenya's Second-in-Command.

Or nothing.

But where was that little bitch?

"Oleg, where's the woman with the camera?" she asked the closest pirate.

He looked like a man having a nightmare about suddenly being back in school to take a pop quiz he hadn't studied for.

Of course, if Oleg had ever studied, he wouldn't have ended up here.

Men. Worthless except for one thing, most of the time.

She growled and headed forward to find Mila. Perhaps the woman had gone that way.

When she found Mila, Zhenya looked around as her Second-in-Command organized pirates emptying out displays.

Something was missing.

"Where's the probe?" Zhenya asked as she got close.

Mila looked around confused for a second. Looked up.

"I'm not sure," she said. "It was with us two chambers back."

Zhenya nodded.

For one or the other to disappear might be coincidental. Both vanishing at once was a problem.

Navarre was up to something.

"Drop everything," Zhenya said. Then she grabbed the nearest male and shoved him towards the door. "Find the blonde. Find Navarre while you're at it. Pass the word."

Her tone and volume were enough to get her men in motion. Many were carrying loot, but that was fine. If this was a trap of some sort, at least they'd escape with a good chunk of the museum's contents. Or at least the valuable bits.

She could always come back later for the rest.

But a voice in her head had her in motion.

Mila started yelling behind her as she left the room, driving more and more of the pirates into Zhenya's direction.

She gathered up several and carried them in her emotional wake.

Out the front door she paused.

"Where are the prisoners?" she demanded, only to be met by shrugs.

Fools.

She'd let Navarre bamboozle her, and her curs had slacked off as a result, letting him do all the work.

"Move it!" she snapped, turning and walking.

Not at a run. Not even a jog. Nothing to suggest panic to the gunslingers and killers around her.

A hard stride, slamming heels angrily down as she went. They picked up on that and hardened their faces.

Out here, things were in normal motion. Men and a few women coming and going, hauling off loot and packing it for flight. Like they'd all done dozens of times before.

"Where's the probe?" she asked as she went by. "Where is the blonde with the camera?"

More shrugs.

Nobody was responsible for the woman, so nobody had bothered tracking her. She'd slipped away when nobody looked.

Golden hair reflecting sunlight caught Zhenya's attention. The blonde.

She began to jog, drawing the pistol she'd largely ignored because there was nobody to shoot at.

Until now.

The distance was extreme, but the small woman was only walking. Zhenya started to run in her wake.

Behind her, the rest of her pirates fell farther and farther behind, unable to keep up.

Or unfaed by the betrayal they didn't sense.

Zhenya let rage fuel her footsteps.

Even farther away, she saw the tall woman who was Navarre's bodyguard. Hadiiye.

If Zhenya had had any doubts, seeing that woman with Navarre and her entire team, including that floating probe, dispersed them.

Zhenya raised her pistol. The range was extreme, but she was closing on the blonde with every stride and would get answers out of her.

Then Zhenya saw movement beyond, as Hadiiye raised her own pistol.

PART 6

Djamila considered the range. The temperature and humidity levels would play a measurable part as she triangulated everything in her head. Suvi's probe was entirely out of effective range.

Stacia McNulty. Approximate range one hundred and eighty meters, closing at a slow walk.

Zhenya Kovalev. Approximate range three hundred meters, closing at an eighteen-second-pace for a one hundred meter dash. Not quite a dead run.

Level terrain. Cover in the form of six starships of various sizes parked between here and there.

Djamila smiled as she lifted her pistol.

Vinogradov's carbine wouldn't have been any better for a shot like this, and Djamila rarely needed to consider engaging at this range with pistols. Had she more time, Djamila might have tasked Iqbal with making the shot, but he was out of position and McNulty had less than a second before Kovalev opened fire at her unsuspecting back.

Djamila centered her weapon and let thirty years of time

on gun ranges align its existence on the pirate. She wasn't looking at the woman, so much as taking in the entire horizon, centered on a moving dot of rage palpable even at this distance.

She fired.

Partial hit, which was in the third standard deviation for such a shot. Not great, but most people would have missed entirely.

Kovalev went to her knees, then face-planted as her legs didn't work all that well.

Partially stunned was almost worse, because you were awake to note how your body stopped responding correctly. Djamila would generally prefer to be out cold.

Except that being awake allowed her to plan. To force numb legs and hands to do as she demanded.

Recovery would improve by fractions, but those fractions might mean the difference between life and death.

Kovalev down unfortunately put her safely out of sight as well, which prevented Djamila from taking a follow-up shot to keep her down.

The shot had been rushed. Tagged the woman high on her right shoulder. Sufficient to save Stacia's life. Not enough to end Kovalev as a threat.

Djamila waved McNulty to start running.

It took the woman another moment and a look back at the mob starting to bay for blood behind her, then McNulty turned into a jackrabbit.

Djamila smiled.

"Defensive fire," she said to her killers. "I need McNulty safely aboard."

"Excessive violence is called for," Javier spoke up. "I'm about to start blowing shit up, so feel free to start early with any explosives you don't want to haul home."

Djamila laughed at the look of sheer joy on Galal's face as he stuffed his pistol into the holster and rotated the grenade launcher off his back, chambered a round, and lofted it into the distance.

Two more joined it before the first landed, detonating on a ship close to the mob of pirates starting to move this way. They panicked and went for cover.

Around her, Djamila's people cut loose with everything they had.

PART 7

Javier nodded to the outgoing barrage and went up the ramp to Mila's ship. No cargo in here yet, but that was because the plan had called for ships closer in to be filled first before taking off for others to replace them.

Mila would normally have landed in the front row, since she flew a big panel van of a ship, but the woman had been carrying a full load of passengers on this trip.

Still, the distance today helped.

Outside, he could hear a shitload of weapons opening up. Bullets started to spang angrily off the hull around him, but nothing was getting through and none of those punks had the sorts of anti-tank firepower they would need to threaten him.

Not until somebody got smart and took off. All those fighters had more than enough guns to do the trick.

He threw himself into the pilot's seat and started a preflight. Most of the checklist he could skip, because she'd done a solid, professional job of shutting it down two hours ago.

The one thing he did that she hadn't done was bring the guns live.

Ship this size had a turret on the bottom, plus four small pulsars on the wings. Parallel rather than parallaxing, but this wasn't a fighter by design. Rather, it was a personnel transport with guns added later.

Good enough for the crazy shit he had planned.

Javier had a count going in his head. Almost to the second, the first set of steps pounded up the ramp.

"Strap yourself in tight!" he yelled, assuming it was Stacia, with everyone else covering her escape and about to pile in behind her.

Instead of listening, she kept coming. He assumed it was her.

Just in case, Javier pulled his pistol and pointed it at her as she got to the doorway.

Stacia yelped and ducked.

"Just making sure," he said. "I said strap in."

"Up here, damn it," she snapped angrily, throwing herself into the co-pilot seat.

And turning that damned camera on him. Should have known.

He'd hired her for a job. She didn't think it was done yet, obviously.

Javier shrugged and slipped back into the Navarre persona for a little while longer.

Aft, more stomping.

"We are clear to lift," Djamila yelled. "Closing the ramp now!"

"Take over the belly turret, someone!" Javier yelled back, then started bringing power to the repulsor collective.

The ship flew like a wasp, hovering delicately in place as the light from aft went out with the ass end finally sealed.

"Stand by for powered flight!" Javier yelled, mostly for the benefit of folks watching the video Stacia was shooting.

Instead of slamming it to the stops and racing for the heavens, Javier set the craft to rotating in place slowly, nose down, counter-clockwise, while he set the forward guns to auto-fire as quickly as the generators could recharge the capacitors.

Below him, he felt the turret spin in place and someone started taking more precise shots at various ships on the ground. Again, mostly just to damage things so that they had to be repaired prior to flight.

The pirates weren't big on skinsuits, so if you had a missing windshield, you had a flight ceiling of about six thousand meters. Unless you wanted to surrender to the local authorities who might be a little bit pissed after all this.

Some of them might have to make that choice soon.

Helped that nobody else had caught on to what was about to happen. No other ships started shooting back, though that would change shortly.

If nothing else, some fool would realize that they'd been betrayed.

And come loaded for bear.

Javier completed one rotation and figured he needed to get gone. This ship wasn't as fast as some of them, and he needed a head start if he wanted to survive this crazy-ass stunt.

He cut the wing guns, adjusted trim and repulsors, then stood this bitch on her ass and finally slammed the thrusters to the stops.

Bye, bye…

PART 8

Stacia watched with her mouth dropped open, but it wouldn't appear on camera at any point, so she could pretend to be as calm, cool, and deadly as the folks around her.

Shocked to her core, however.

She'd been filming Navarre, but watching on the targeting screen as he blew up a number of ships on the ground. Plus someone in the turret was doing the same, even as the ship was suddenly tilted backwards and racing to the heavens.

Navarre laughed under his breath at some joke unshared.

"Gunner, got a target coming in from the southwest," he announced.

"Already noted," Hadiiye replied with a yell. "Letting them get closer."

Navarre nodded and kept flying.

"What's happening, Captain Navarre?" Stacia asked.

She could voiceover all this later, but it would be better coming from the horse's mouth. Or something.

"While taking off, we damaged a number of those ships," he replied, glancing over. "They can lift off, but will not make it to orbit without repairs because they are no longer vacuum-rated. You can land in the middle of nowhere and try, but most probably don't have the tools to effect repairs. And an angry planet looking for them. Then, we stole this one. Hadiiye is about to open fire on somebody chasing us. There it goes. And boom. Idiot forgot we were armed and was flying straight and level. He's dead. More coming, but they'll be strung out in a line rather than massed. Big difference. And pissed at me, so they might not be thinking straight."

"Did you kill Captain Kovalev?" she asked, flashing back in terror to the shot that she seemed to feel zip right past her.

"Hadiiye, is Kovalev dead?" he yelled.

"Negative, Navarre," the big killer yelled back. "Stun settings and I didn't want to take time to adjust."

"There you go," the man nodded at her. "Boss bitch will be leading a mob baying for my blood. Doubly so as I stole Mila's ship and have no intention of giving it back. Angry ladies."

"Now what?" Stacia asked.

It was all a blur, even in the middle of things. The ping from Suvi to leave. The sudden appearance of a mob of killers chasing her. Firefight in the middle of the landing field. Taking off but shooting everything first.

Finally, a moonshot straight up.

"Now, we get gone," Navarre said. "Lot of them are faster than we are. Thrust/weight ratios favor kids in stripped-down sleds over trucks with a big crew. Head start helps. Gunner firing in back helps, as they have to maneuver to stay away from her."

"Is that why you are slowly spiraling upwards?" Stacia asked.

She was concentrating on keeping her lunch down, but the motion wasn't that bad. Mostly in her head. She was not a hardened pirate.

Not like the lunatics around her, even as much as they had accepted her as one of them.

"That's right," he replied to her question. "Hadiiye can keep firing at anyone trying to get on my blind side for a clean shot. Again, slows me down, but all I need to do is get away. JumpDrives, if nothing else. But I've got a few more tricks up my sleeve."

"Such as?"

"You'll see," Navarre winked at the camera.

She knew the look in his eyes and let it go. He had something special, and wasn't about to say anything, even to her while she was filming.

Hopefully, it would keep her alive so she could actually make the documentary she'd been planning.

PART 9

Zhenya hadn't even wiped the mud and muck from her face from where that bitch had shot her and dropped her to face plant. She'd grabbed Mila and they had raced to her own ship, taking off as soon as they could.

Around them, power plants and fuel stores exploded from where Navarre and his betrayal had opened fire, both with small arms as well as Mila's ship.

"Strap yourselves down!" Zhenya called as she got into her seat. "Lifting now."

Mila was aft somewhere, as there was only the one seat in the cockpit. Zhenya's.

A turret gunner, a navigator, a cook. And her Second-in-Command.

Zhenya skipped most of her preflight and lifted off immediately. Around her, a few ships even managed to crash into each other as they did so, damaging both and usually falling onto a third or even fourth with secondary damage and some explosions.

Navarre had picked the absolute worst moment to betray her. He had to have known that. Planned for it.

She would make him pay in blood.

Zhenya had the fastest ship in the squadron. By design. She tilted it backwards and pushed the engines as far as they would go. Slow for now, but accelerating from a dead stop.

Ahead of her, an explosion marked a ship disintegrating. One of hers, as she could just make out the tiny dot that was Navarre, fleeing from her like a rabbit.

Wouldn't be enough. She would have his head on a stake in her throne room as a warning to the next fool who thought to challenge her.

Zhenya flipped to a rear camera and cursed at the damage on the ground. More explosions. More crashed ships. Likely half her people weren't getting home from this catastrophe, because the locals would be seeing blood.

Worse, they'd only barely begun to load stolen loot. She had to wonder how few of the ships finally starting to launch in her wake had any cargo at all. Packing usually took several hours, and everyone was following her.

Probably just as well. Mila would have needed to be on the ground to coordinate something, and she was at least as angry as Zhenya.

They would make Navarre pay.

PART 10

Javier watched that one dot creeping closer on his rear scanner. Mila had invested in decent hardware. Nothing great, but most of the ships behind him barely had navigational computers worth the name. Short range sensors were usually eyeballs more than anything, relying on command ships like this one for anything more exotic.

He'd missed hitting Kovalev's ship. Luck of the draw on rotation. Might have been a mistake, not to make sure.

And might not. Hard to say.

"Hadiiye, can you hit her?" he called.

There really shouldn't be much doubt as to who he was talking about. Kovalev was closest. And closing fastest. Whole freaking mob of angry ugliness behind her. On his scanner, they looked like geese in an arrowhead formation, but that was a two-dimensional display. They were far more haphazard on the camera view.

"Only if you flew so perfectly still that the rest of them could shoot back," Hadiiye answered.

Like that was a smart idea.

He nodded. Then turned to Stacia and her camera.

"We keep dodging so they can't line us up for a shot," he explained for her future viewers. "Keeps us safe, but lets them catch up, because they are flying in straight lines. We've got a lead, but she's eating it slowly away with every kilometer everyone climbs. Fortunately, we're already past the technical edge of the atmosphere, which is one hundred kilometers for legal purposes on most planets. Got a ways to go, though."

He waited for her to press, but Stacia just nodded. Waiting.

There would be all sorts of explanations dubbed over later, but that was the nature of the beast.

He'd watched enough nature documentaries to understand that he was the fox today, and Kovalev the hound.

Gonna be close, too.

"Navarre, you'll never escape me," Kovalev's voice was suddenly there on the comm. "You can run, you son of a bitch, but you'll never run far enough. Mila and I will hunt you to the ends of the universe."

Even *sounded* like Fryda on a bad day. Which was one of the reasons Javier had a second *ex*-wife.

He didn't bother replying. It would come across as macho bullshit or taunting, and he was on camera.

Javier kept flying.

"How long until she catches us?" Stacia asked after a pause.

"Thirty seconds, probably," Javier replied. "If I let her. Figure she's close enough. And angry enough. Never let it be said that I don't know how to piss off a woman. Got two ex-wives I will not get you in touch with to verify that. I have hopefully learned better, but some skills you only learn much later."

He looked over and got the perfectly arched eyebrow that every mother apparently teaches her daughters when they are about to hit teenager.

Javier grinned. Then he opened a comm line.

"Suvi, we're in Mila's ship with a posse on our asses," he announced. "Tell me you've got my back."

"You're late, actually," his favorite daughter replied laconically. "We were beginning to wonder if maybe you'd gotten a better offer on the ground or something."

Javier couldn't help the laughter that erupted. Felt good to be alive.

"Captain Kovalev is the closest ship behind me," he said.

"Yup," Suvi cut him off. "Been watching her and wondering if she was good enough to catch you."

"I'd prefer not finding out," Javier retorted. "Could you folks maybe do something about all this?"

"Hey, dork," Mary-Elizabeth was suddenly on the line. "'Bout time you joined the party."

Javier's grin felt a kilometer wide.

"*Surayya* Defense Forces, this is *Concord* Warship Captain Sokolov aboard *Excalibur*," Zakhar came over the general comm. "Target designated *Alpha* is friendly. All others are fair game. Engage as you bear."

Javier dialed his forward scanners wider and noticed a sudden cloud of smaller ships coming out from *Excalibur*'s shadow. Twenty-one of them. Scan read them as orbital defense fighters.

Hawks, about to feast on pigeons.

"Yee-HAW!!!!" Javier whooped. Then he turned to the camera, so posterity would understand. "I'm not sure how, but Zakhar talked the locals into helping out and hiding above him in orbit. They have just turned into the cavalry that's going to save our asses, because nothing coming after us right now can challenge them."

"Why not?" Stacia asked.

Javier flipped to rear scanners and tapped the screen for her to turn her camera.

"That's only about half the horde," he noted. "The other

half didn't lift off. Maybe can't. Maybe trapped on the planet. The rest didn't launch as a unit, but instead as fast as anybody could give chase, so they are a line of mice about to be swallowed by a hungry snake."

"What about Captain Kovalev?" Stacia asked.

The gods were obviously favoring Stacia today, because at that exact moment somebody—Mary-Elizabeth or Suvi—hit Kovalev's ship with a single pulsar. The explosion felt huge, but that was only in his mind. More like a can of beer being crushed underfoot than anything.

Still, decapitated chicken, on top of everything else.

Excalibur opened fire with the rest of her pulsars.

Then the hawks began their dive.

Javier tapped Stacia on the knee and got the camera tilted back to him.

"The Pirate Horde of *Syntha* is done," he said to the camera with as much dignity and finality as he could manage. "A few might escape me today, but not many. And their leaders are now dead, so anyone who does flee will have to start over. If *Valadris* was smart, they'd send a military detachment to *Syntha* as soon as possible to arrest everybody and confiscate anything that wasn't nailed down."

"That's not you?" Stacia asked.

"I was—we were—hired to destroy the pirate horde by some lovely folks from *Byormi*," Navarre-the-killer said to eternity. "I get to go tell them the good news, as soon as I drop you off at home."

He turned back to the cloud of expanding gas that represented Zhenya and Mila, being joined by lots of others as Sokolov's friends cut loose.

Yeah. It felt good to be alive.

EPILOGUE

Javier hadn't planned it, but folks had insisted, so his team had ridden down to the surface of *Byormi* dressed in their finest pirate regalia. Not just him and Djamila, either. Adrian had worked up a uniform scheme for the Gunbunnies and the Pathfinders. Plus Zakhar had gotten into the act.

Maroon seemed to be a thing. Luck of the draw, really, because 'Mina had originally put it together on the fly from ship's stores on *Storm Gauntlet*. And it was weird, not seeing Zakhar in green.

Hadiiye stood out in purple, but again, by design.

Around them, a mob of maroon dissolved into a sea of color as the party got going. *Byormi* was a poor world. Lots of them were. Rich in people and land. And dreams.

Not a lot of cash.

Suited him fine. He'd done this job for six *Concord* drachmas and a cow. Because how often did you get to tell people that sort of bullshit and have it not only be one hundred percent true, but backed up by everyone else there?

The cow was dinner. He'd insisted on having it slaughtered by a professional and turned into the centerpiece of the party. Two pigs and a lot of other donated critters had joined it.

Somewhere off to his right, a string quartet started up with reels and folks started dancing, but Javier was all about some prime rib right now. And potatoes stuffed with all the fixings. He'd even managed to convince Chay and Burdine to take the night off and fly down with the sisters. Not to cook, but to celebrate.

And maybe buy some more cows, pigs, goats, and whatever else they decided they wanted. He had space on various decks for pens and yards. Or maybe they'd immediately turn into future meals and be hauled up as frozen carcasses that *Excalibur* bought, injecting more cash into the local economy.

Nita Reeves stepped out from the crowd and grabbed him before he could react. Not that he would have put up much of a fight for the kiss she seemed insistent on. Went on longer than probably appropriate, but who was he to judge? He was in Rome, and this might be the Roman way to say hello.

Eventually, she let go. Enough to wrap an arm around him and he got to see Cornell Hawthorne and an older woman standing close.

"Marlene Garnett, it is my pleasure to introduce you to Doctor Javier Aritza, of King's College on *Altai*," Nita said in a bright, cheery voice that made Javier's day better just to hear. "The man who destroyed Zhenya Kovalev."

Not be outdone, the woman stepped up and kissed him. Fifty, from the skin around the eyes, but not hard years. Laughing years, maybe. And a lot more energy than he'd been expecting. Nice looking. Nice bod. Great smile.

Might have to stay a couple of extra days, if the welcome was going to be like that.

Then, to be a shit, he turned and pointed at Zakhar, standing close with Djamila in her Hadiiye outfit between them.

"Technically, Zakhar Sokolov destroyed her," Javier laughed. "I was just the bait and the con man."

Zakhar didn't react fast enough, so Marlene grabbed him for a matching kiss. Took the man a moment to just run with it, even as Djamila rolled her eyes at the entire thing.

Eventually, he got untangled.

"Think food would be good," Zakhar announced, practically dragging Djamila off. Cornell followed, and Javier found himself with the two local women.

Around him, the crew he'd brought down was dancing, eating, and telling tall tales, to see a group of youngsters clustered around Del as he held court.

Marlene pulled a small bag from a pocket. She was in simple slacks and a sweater, though the weather wasn't that cold. Didn't appear to be wearing anything under it, either, and the knit was tight across her in places that drew the eye.

She smiled as she handed him the bag.

"Six *Concord* drachmas," she said with a chuckle. "Finding said coins was something of a pain in the ass, so you might check dates. Couple of them could be antiques worth more than face value."

"Not ever spending them," Javier nodded. "These will go home with us as trophies. Reminders of *Byormi*, *Valadris*, and *Syntha*."

"And you intend to leave forever?" Marlene asked.

She had a disappointed air about her. As did Nita.

"We dropped Stacia McNulty off on the way here," he nodded. "I expect you'll meet her eventually, but I refused to carry her here because she needed to get her people into motion with the information she brought home. She will come here. I will be gone around the curve of the galaxy by then."

"*Altai*?" Nita asked.

"Eventually, we're going home, but not yet," he nodded. "Or rather, not that fast. Taking the time to do a few things first."

"Nita told me some bits about *Umen* and *Ormint*," Marlene said. "She didn't understand why you do such things. Especially not for so little. The risks do not seem to balance the rewards."

Javier paused to obviously ogle both women, which they seemed to be inviting, then he turned serious.

"I'll leave you with a copy of a manuscript," he said. "One of my old professors calls it *The Rising Storm* and expects another major war to break out in the next generation or so. Bigger than the Great War that functionally destroyed *Neu Berne*, *Balustrade*, and the *Union of Man* and catapulted the *Concord* into hegemony. Much worse. Wider. Deadlier. Something about trends in human civilization that can be tracked with predictive value."

"You expect that war to reach us here?" Nita asked.

"I expect it to reach everyone, eventually," Javier replied. "For some, it will be a devastating hurricane, while others might only feel a kiss of breeze on their cheek in passing. What I told McNulty was that this region of space would only be able to resist and survive it if *Valadris* got their acts together and got rid of all the corruption. That included *Syntha*. For places like *Byormi*, you'll have to keep building, then expect to support *Valadris* later. Maybe all of you joined together as a single nation that might be strong enough."

"Do you know when?" Marlene asked.

"I do not," Javier shook his head. "Dorn seems to think not less than one generation, but not more than three. So twenty-five to seventy-five years. I'll be home on *Altai* retired, either way, but my job is to make sure that other worlds have a chance to build stronger walls while they can."

"That is a depressing thought," Marlene said. "That children today might live to see it. Fight in it, even. And there is nothing we can do?"

"We can prepare," Javier said. "Tonight, that means celebrating new friends."

He held out a hand and Marlene took it, even as Nita kept her grip on his hip.

"Tomorrow you'll be gone?" Marlene asked.

"Tomorrow," he said.

She stepped close and kissed him again.

"Then perhaps tonight should be something special," she murmured.

Javier smiled.

He couldn't save everyone, but he could damned sure try.

READ MORE

To read more of my fiction, sign up for my newsletter. You'll also get a free book!

http://www.blazeward.com/newsletter/

READ MORE

To read more of my fiction, sign up for my newsletter. You'll also get a free book!

http://www.blazeward.com/newsletter/

ABOUT THE AUTHOR

Blaze Ward is a prolific Indie writer and publisher who works mostly in Science Fiction and Light Thriller, with occasional forays into lots of other genres like superheroic fantasy.

You can find more of his titles at www.blazeward.com/books, www.KnottedRoadPress.com and wherever else you buy your books.

He also edits Boundary Shock Quarterly, an SF magazine he founded in 2018, and Thrill Ride Magazine.

ABOUT KNOTTED ROAD PRESS

Knotted Road Press publishes dynamic fiction set in exotic locations. Our authors cover a wide range of genres including science fiction, fantasy, mystery, literary, and poetry. We also have unique non-fiction voices in genres such as autobiography, business, cookbooks, and how-tos. We offer both DRM-free ebooks and print books for a global readership.

www.KnottedRoadPress.com